Tanya Stern
The Troubadour

Tanya Stern

THE TROUBADOUR

translated from the German
by Margaret Vallance

Part of the Series
OPERA MURDER

Stern, Tanya: The Troubadour
translated from the German by Margaret Vallance
Part of the Series OPERA MURDER
1nd edition 2017
ISBN 978-3-938105-28-3
cover: Tanya Stern
title image: Johann Heinrich Füssli, The Nightmare (1781)
(source: www.zeno.org - Zenodot Verlagsgesellschaft mbH)

Part One
The Count's Legacy

I

Not far from Zaragoza, on a hill close by the small town of A., the sombre ruin of a castle can be seen, its weathered and craggy walls half broken down after centuries of neglect. The peasants call it the 'Castillo de Luna', and impress upon any inquisitive stranger that once upon a time this desolate place exercised a power that was felt in even the most remote villages of the area. Count Alvaro de Luna, who once gave his name to the castle, was a remarkable man. In his youth he had accompanied Pedro the Fourth on his military campaigns and was one of the first to set foot in the besieged citadel of Trinacria. It was thanks to this and many other heroic deeds that he acquired the title of Count, as well as the Castillo near Zaragoza, which the grateful Prince gave to him. It was in this Castillo that the Count, having sacrificed his youth and health in the service of the Empire, intended to spend his twilight years enjoying well-earned leisure and prosperity. He chose a beautiful bride from amongst the daughters of the nobility, and established a grand estate at A. with a multitude of servants and his own private garrison. Where now wild grass grows through the cracks in the walls there were once held magnificent balls – where now the only sound to be heard is the monotonous chirping of the cicadas, once you could hear shouts and the clattering of horses' hooves. In the course of time two fine sons were born in the Castillo and the happiness of the family appeared to be complete.

However, one summer a troupe of travelling players came by – minstrels and jugglers, who performed in the market places. Gaily costumed dancers displayed their skill with tambourines and castanets. There was a fool, a fire-eater and an old gypsy woman who read people's fortunes from their palms. News of the arrival of these players soon reached the ears of the Count, and as new forms of diversion were a rarity in those times, he invited the whole troupe to his Castillo for the purpose of entertaining his guests after the hunt.

It was a mild summer's evening, so the performance took place in the open air. No sooner had the guests gathered together in the inner courtyard and the musicians begun to play, accompanied by the rattle of tambourines, when there was a disturbance. At first this seemed to be of little consequence; and yet it was to bring great misery to more than one family. The old gypsy woman, who was wandering amongst the guests, offering to tell their fortunes, began to attract the attention of Nuño, the Count's first-born son, a high spirited boy, about six years of age. The boy found her old-fashioned clothes, her eccentric gestures and her strange dialect amusing. He made mockery of her, following her around, plucking at her skirts, mimicking her gruff manner of speech. When she angrily shooed him away, he picked up a horsewhip and threw it in front of her, causing her to stumble over it, falling flat on her face on the ground - giving rise to much merriment on the part of the guests standing around, and to Nuño's great amusement.

The old gypsy woman gathered herself up and while the onlookers slapped their thighs with delight, shot a look at the boy of such fury that it seemed almost physical in its violence.

'Look at that' she spoke in a cracking voice, 'the little Count – so young and already so full of contempt for an old woman! Give me your hand!' she barked at him, stretching her own bony hand towards him. 'I will tell your fortune and not demand a penny for it!'

The laughter died away and little Nuño turned pale, backing away from her and hiding his hands behind his back. He felt as though the old woman's eyes were penetrating his innermost soul. She stood, stretched up to her full height, pointing her arm at him, and began to speak vehemently: 'Forget about your hand, little Count, in your case I have no need of it. I know full well what your future holds. You were born with many gifts, yet you will have no joy of them. You will be rich, but you will never possess that which you most desire. You will live to be old, but you will envy those who die young. Where you win you will lose and where you love you will kill. You will be accursed till the end of your life!'

With these words she turned away and hobbled off, yet with her head held high.

The guests looked at each other in dismay. The gypsy woman had spoken with such power of conviction that she did not fail to make a profound impression upon all who heard her. Even little Nuño understood, if not her actual words, at least the meaning of her look, her tone of voice, her commanding presence, and he was filled with a deep sense of dread. He ran to his father, trembling all over, begging him to protect him from the 'wicked witch'. But the Count, busy with his duties as host, and unable to make much sense of the child's stammering words, laughingly dismissed the story as the foolish gabble of a crazy old woman. He ordered the nursemaid to put his son to bed, and continued with the evening's entertainment.

But soon he had cause to change his mind. The trembling that had started when Nuño heard the gypsy's words, continued through the night. Worse: it turned into a high fever and by the following day the child lay hovering between life and death. The Count sent at once for doctors, but all their attempts to bring the fever down were in vain. As the feverish boy restlessly threw himself to and fro upon his pillows he was tormented by fantasies featuring the 'wicked witch' who had 'wounded him with her eyes'. And in truth, was it not this that had happened? Surely the hateful old woman was to blame for Nuño's illness? Had she not aimed her poisonous look and her evil words at the boy?

At any rate, this was how the family of the Count began to regard the matter. The doctor expressed a similar opinion. Weeping, his distraught mother, seeing her son's life ebbing away with each day that passed, demanded that the heathen woman be punished. The prior of the nearby monastery, an authority on religious matters, made so bold as to propound the view that the boy would only be cured once the body of the guilty person had been burned at the stake.

Therefore to the Count this left only one possible interpretation of the events. He sent his caballeros out to seek the players and to apprehend the person guilty of causing his son's malady.

A few days later the old woman was brought to the castle in chains. At first she vehemently denied her crime, maintaining that she had not done anything to bring about the catastrophe, merely foretelling that it would come to pass. It had been imposed by a higher power. Only when put to the most extreme forms of torture did she finally admit to having bewitched the Count's son, and to having laid a curse upon him.

Now it was necessary to make all haste to commit the witch's body to the purifying fire – every day that passed could cost Nuño his life. This prospect made the Count harden his heart. In vain did the daughter of the gypsy woman, with a young child of her own in her arms, manage to evade the guards and make her way into his bed chamber, where she threw herself in desperation at his feet, begging him to show mercy to her old mother. The Count, concerned only for the safety of his son, turned her from his door.

Barely a week after the gypsy woman had been apprehended, a stake was erected and ceremoniously lit in the market place of A. The Count appeared with his family; even his sick son, Nuño, was carried there in a litter, as the doctor had assured the family that this would have a beneficial effect. The prior issued forth from the monastery followed by his monks and the craftsmen and peasants came out of their houses, just as only a short while before they had come out to watch the merry group of players, and amongst them the very woman who was this day led before them in chains, now disfigured by the torture she had endured, filthy and sick. With bowed head, offering no resistance, she let them bind her to the stake. Ignoring the waiting crowd, ignoring the Count and his family who were the cause of her suffering, ignoring even her own daughter who stood right at the front of the crowd of avid spectators, weeping and holding up her grandson towards her. It was as if death could only come as deliverance for this tormented creature.

But as the flames began to devour her, she uttered a scream that caused all around her to shudder. Her eyes appeared to search amongst the crowd of onlookers as if she were seeking a kindred soul, and now at last, she recognised her daughter. The onlookers saw her body writhe in agony and suddenly they heard her howls turn into words. At first they could not comprehend the words. The smoke distorted her voice, which was already hoarse and broken by her suffering, and the crackling of the flamed threatened to drown her words. Yet when she cried out repeatedly, the same words, over and over again, every one of those present in the square that day understood them. 'Avenge me!' she cried out to her daughter, and again, and yet again: 'Avenge me! Avenge me!' She screamed these words as long as she could draw breath, and all those who heard them felt their blood turn to ice. Then at last her head fell forward, her cries faded away, she was no more.

Slowly the peasants left the scene. The monks, murmuring prayers as they went, followed their prior back to their monastery and the Count and his family betook themselves to their coaches. One figure remained standing there, that of the gypsy woman's daughter. She stood there alone, together with her small son, and she remained standing there until long after the fire had died down and the body of her mother had burned away into a blackened lump. She stayed there until dusk fell, staring at the cold cinders, in her arms her child whimpering with hunger. However, when morning came she had vanished without trace.

II

As the weeks passed, the prior's prophecy appeared to be miraculously fulfilled. Nuño recovered, albeit very slowly, and the family breathed a sigh of relief when at last he was able to take his seat at the table. They began to believe that calamity had been averted; yet there is a kind of calamity that is akin to a pestilence, bringing ever more, ever greater calamities in its wake. By the morning following the harvest festival, Nuño was fully recovered, his mother joyfully entered the nursery, only to find that her younger son, Garcia, then barely two years old, was no longer in his cot. They searched every nook and cranny of the castle. The child had vanished.

Now the search was extended to the grounds, to the entire surrounding district, and enquiries revealed that a peasant from A. as well as one of the Count's huntsmen had both espied a woman, a stranger, who had been lurking in the woods not far from the Castillo. She had appeared to be avoiding all human contact. Neither of them was able to give an exact description of the woman, but it became apparent that this could be none other than the daughter of the cursed gypsy woman. Unforgettable was the terrifying call for vengeance as the mother expired – was this now the daughter's vengeance?

The first indications suggested that this was the case. They found a gap in the outer wall, through which she could easily have slipped – indeed, she had probably used it once already, when she had visited the Count and implored him to show mercy towards her mother. The Count recalled his own amazement, that the woman had been able to evade the guards and find her way undetected to his private chamber. Now he realised to his horror: the witch's daughter knew the way into his home and thus the way to his heart. There seemed to him to be something deeply calculating about the way in which she had robbed him of Garcia, his innocent young son: for he had been the apple of his parents' eyes, their pride and joy, an unusually keen-witted and gifted child who gave rise to great promise.

Would they be in time to apprehend the woman who had stolen

their child before she was able to wreak her revenge? Like her mother, she had belonged to the group of travelling players, the source of all this misery. She had been a singer there and the Count had been struck by her dark, slightly throaty voice when she had performed before his guests upon that fateful evening, when her fate was to cross his. For the second time, he commanded his caballeros to seek out the players once more, and to interrogate each of them most rigorously, but to no avail. When her mother had been seized, the daughter had likewise left the group, and none of her companions had seen or heard anything of her again. The Count sent forth search parties to comb the woods. In every village and hamlet he had notices put up, announcing the theft of his child and giving a description of the wanted woman. He offered such a huge reward that within a short time each and every woman travelling with a small child had been closely examined, even subjected to ill-treatment. But they could find no trace of the woman they sought.

Days and weeks passed, during which the family suffered the torment of uncertainty. The entire Castillo was plunged into deep melancholy. The Countess, torn between hope and despair, lay sick with a nervous fever. It was then that a peasant made a grim discovery. Close by a stream that flowed only a few miles away from the town of A. he found the remnants of a campfire containing the remains of human bones – the bones of a small child. The Count's caballeros, called thither, carried out a thorough search of the cold ashes and the surrounding area and discovered in the bushes the torn stocking of a child, which, without a shadow of a doubt, had been that of Garcia, the wretched Count's son. The case was clear: the gypsy woman had carried out her mother's final wishes by shedding Garcia's innocent blood.

The news of the child's murder spread like wildfire throughout the countryside, causing great outrage. There were attacks upon gypsy encampments. When they brought the news to the Countess, she sank down, lifeless, upon her couch. She lived for only a few weeks longer, grief-stricken, her spirit broken. And by the time she was borne to her grave the Count himself was no longer the man he had once been. Instead of entertaining on a lavish scale he spent his evenings sitting alone by the fireside. Instead of going out hunting he would spend whole days at a time, locked in his private chapel, indulging in a bizarre form of death cult. For he had the charred bones of his son preserved in a special chamber, and it was here that the old man would sit for hours at a time, gazing at the bones, which had once been his joy, his hope and the pride of his house. He could barely bring himself to be separated from them. In vain did his friends remind him that he still had one son remaining to him, that he owed duties as a father to Nuño, who, although growing up as a healthy boy, was visibly marked by the tragic events. For the Count he could not replace the loved ones he had lost. Upon occasion it even seemed as if the Count were holding his elder son to blame for his misery, as if he were beginning to harbour in his heart a dislike for the boy.

With the passing of the years the old man's worship of the dead took on ever more bizarre forms. Thus, one day, he commenced measuring Garcia's bones, his holy relics, with the aid of a ruler, and then examining them minutely. He consulted learned doctors and read texts books on anatomy, reaching the surprising conclusion that the bones that had been found in the fire could not possibly be those of Garcia, that they must have been those of a much younger child, at most one year old. He based his conclusion in particular on one upper thigh bone, which had remained virtually intact.

He proclaimed this theory to everyone who visited him, but none could share his conviction. They would listen politely to his long-winded explanations of body structure and bone measurement, but behind his back they would shake their heads. They were to believe that Garcia might still be alive? And all the melancholy pieces of evidence, fitted perfectly to prove exactly the opposite? What could the measurements of half cremated bones divulge? All those who knew him, including his own son, took him to be a deranged old man, to be pitied, overcome by the merciless blows of fate, in the grip of an obsession.

The old man perceived that people did not believe him, but this failed to shake his firm conviction that Garcia was alive. On the contrary, the older and more infirm he became, the stronger grew this inner conviction. It was not even the anatomical measurements that filled him with such certainty. They had merely served to strengthen what his feelings as a father were telling him. Garcia was alive – somewhere in the world he was growing up into a youth, indeed into manhood. But what did this knowledge avail the father? Was not his son, though merely lost, just as distant from him as if he were dead?

This was his grief, this quiet despair that gnawed at his heart and hastened his old age. He had barely reached the age of sixty when one morning he was struck down on the stairs by a stroke, which caused paralysis in every limb. But even on his deathbed he attempted to impress upon Nuño with all the strength his failing powers allowed him, his unassailable conviction that his second son was yet among the living, and he beseeched the youth to be constantly mindful of this belief.

These were almost the last words that the Count spoke. A few hours later he lost consciousness and by the evening of the same day his soul had departed.

III

Don Nuño, who was now eighteen years old, did not entertain the slightest doubt that his brother was dead, despite his dying father's insistence that he still lived. Although his father's final words had deeply affected him, they did not linger long in his mind. The dead man's last wish was sacred to him, but what could he do to fulfil it? Even if it were true that Garcia was alive, he was surely lost to the family for ever. Don Nuño had no desire to follow his father's example and grieve over a phantom.

He was now the sole heir to the Castillo, all the property and the title of Count, and despite his youth, he felt himself more than capable of administering his estate, and of upholding the honour of his family. Over the years that followed, he refurbished the Castillo in A. and added many acquisitions. Furthermore, as his father had done before him, he would arrange great hunting parties and host grand balls, participating in jousting tournaments, with con-

siderable success, and was a popular guest in the grand houses
of the surrounding countryside. Thus many a noble family would
have been glad to welcome this self-assured young man as a son-
in-law. However, his taste was hard to satisfy, and he made such
high demands of any future Countess de Luna that no young lady
of his acquaintance met his high expectations.

In the course of time, he duly became an army officer, like his
father. Following the death of King Martin I, a dispute had broken
out between Ferdinand, the Prince of Castile and the ambitious
Count of d'Urgell over the crown of Aragón. Although the Prince's
Crown Council had declared in favour of Ferdinand, the Count of
d'Urgell refused to accept this decision and had attempted to gain
by force of arms what the judges had denied him. The Pretender
to the throne of Castile knew that right was on his side, yet there
were many citizens of Aragón who resented the dominian of the
House of Castile, and were sympathetic to the cause of the rebellious Count, either openly or in secret. This had already led to
confrontations and even to skirmishes between the two parties.
There was an imminent threat of a bloody civil war, the duration
and outcome of which was uncertain.

It was natural that Don Nuño should fight in support of Fernando, the rightful heir to the throne, and due to his family con-
nections as well as his natural talent as a leader, he soon rose to
a high rank in the royal army. Here also there were those who
courted his friendship, particularly among the younger officers,
but here also he proved hard to please, and accepted only a very
few as worthy companions.

There was only one with whom he entered into a close relationship: a captain by the name of Guillén de Sesé. Not that he
could boast of noble descent, as could Don Nuño. Following the
early death of his father, the family fortune, which had been considerable, had dwindled to almost nothing. Yet what Don Guillén
lacked in money and influence, he made up for with personal bra-
very and burning ambition. He regarded it to be his goal in life to
restore the family's fortune and position in society, and he pursued this goal with such zeal that Don Nuño could not help but
respect him for it.

When they found themselves encamped near Zaragoza, the Easter festival was approaching, and Don Guillén invited his friend to spend the holiday with him at the de Sesé family estate not far from T. Don Nuño, who had nothing better to do, agreed at once, and so, on Maundy Thursday the two friends took leave from their duties and set off on horseback in the direction of T.

It was not long, however, before Don Nuño had reason to rue his decision. Until then he had known only that Don Guillén's widowed mother and younger sister lived on the estate towards which they were riding. But now the captain began to describe his family in more detail. Indeed, he spoke mainly about his sister: that she was eighteen years old, that she had grown up in a convent and had only been living at home again during the past year, but that within this short period of time her exceptional beauty had made her the object of much admiration, that she was shortly to attend court as a lady in waiting to the Infanta Maria... Don Guillén related all this with a brother's justifiable pride, but there was an undertone to his remarks that awakened the Count's suspicion. Could there be a delicate reason behind the Easter invitation beyond that of comradeship? If that is the case, my dear fellow, thought he to himself, casting a sideways glance at the captain, then I will sorely disappoint you and your family. I have no intention of choosing the daughter of an impoverished provincial nobleman to be the Countess de Luna, though she be as beautiful as an angel. All you will achieve is that this visit will cause embarrassment to both parties and will put a strain on our relationship.

They reached their destination late in the evening. The de Sesé's family estate was a fairly large building of Moorish style situated in a pretty setting between gentle hills and surrounded by spacious parkland. The travellers were welcomed by Don Guillén's mother, Doña Clara de Sesé, who had stayed up in order to greet the guests, the younger lady of the house having already retired. Doña Clara was exactly as the Count had imagined her: a faded, though carefully dressed lady, who had seen better times and who had not given up the hope of regaining them. In the very first conversation, despite its brevity due to the lateness of the hour,

she alluded several times to her daughter, singing her praises in
a manner that displeased Don Nuño greatly. The house also displeased him, the drawing room with its tattered finery, and the
guestroom into which he was led. Everywhere he thought he
could perceive a desperate attempt to maintain a façade, and a
struggle to appear better than they were. He took himself to bed,
full of resentment, regretting that he had ever accepted the invitation.

IV

Yet the following morning, when he was at last introduced to
Doña Leonor, he was pleasantly surprised. He had expected a
younger version of the obsequious mother, a doll-like creature,
decked out in her best clothes, ambitious, casting languishing
looks at him. But now he was forced to admit that Don Guillén
had not exaggerated. His sister was indeed an exceptionally beautiful girl. Even at court she had provoked admiration, with her
delicate, pale face that had the charm of a half-opened bud, her
gleaming black hair and her almond shaped eyes in which there
shone a dark glimpse of fire. Her expression was serious and demure and her manner was totally free of frivolous vanity and the
desire to please. During breakfast she frequently gazed dreamily
through the window into the grounds, as if she were far away in
her thoughts; and later, during the service in the village church,
which Don Nuño attended with the family, she sank down in devoted prayer and seemed to forget all that was around her. Naturally he told himself that she was merely putting on an act to
impress him with her piety. Yet, each time that he stole a glance
at her, as she knelt by his side, he observed nothing to justify this
suspicion. If she really were acting, then it was a most impressive
and convincing performance. Her lips moved in a whisper and
there was a far away look in her shining eyes. What could she be
asking of her God? What hidden depths were glowing beneath
this well-bred exterior?

The Count looked forward to the evening with some anticipation, hoping to hold a more intimate conversation with Doña Leonor. Even at dinner there was nothing to suggest that she shared her family's hopes, or even that she was aware of them. After the meal the company sat outside on the terrace, where it was still pleasantly warm even at this late hour. While Doña Clara called for liqueurs and Turkish coffee to be served, the young people began to converse about the latest developments in the Aragonese civil war.

With secret astonishment the Count observed the lively interest shown by Doña Leonor in this unsuitable subject. Indeed, it had been she herself who had introduced it, by casually enquiring of the gentlemen as to the latest news of the war; and while the Count provided her with this information she looked at him with a compassionate concern in her beautiful eyes such as he had never seen before. Her questions and remarks revealed a thorough knowledge of the political situation and a tendency to hold firm opinions; she was not afraid of expressing contrary views. When, for instance, Don Guillén declared his loathing of Count d'Urgell, who had attempted to secure the crown by murdering the Archbishop, Doña Leonor expressed doubt as to whether d'Urgell had actually been the initiator of the murderous attack. In her view a man of his political experience would have had the sense to foresee the extent to which this treacherous attack must have damaged his cause.

Doña Clara rebuked her daughter. The gentleman had come, she pointed out with a flattering simper at the Count, to enjoy a few days rest from their arduous military duties, and Leonor, instead of conversing pleasantly with them, was only reminding them of the horrors from which they had flown.

The conversation then turned to more peaceful issues, and Doña Leonor appeared to have lost any further interest in the matter. Once again she gazed dreamily out into the grounds and again the Count had the sensation that she was totally oblivious to his presence. It was not yet ten o'clock when she stood up and begged the company to excuse her, claiming to have a headache. In vain did her mother and brother entreat her to stay, noticing the Count's disappointment. Doña Leonor remained deaf to all entreaties and withdrew immediately to her room, leaving the others on the terrace in some dismay.

Don Nuño was no longer in any doubt. Whatever hopes the de Sesés had cherished from this visit, the main person involved knew nothing of them. Meanwhile Doña Clara, quick to take advantage of her daughter's absence, drew her chair close to that of the Count and began talking to him about Doña Leonor: of how her father had died, when she was a delicate child of seven years; and how she had been admitted to the convent school of the Carmelites, not far from Zaragoza; how she had benefited from an excellent education there and over the years had become the Abbess's favourite pupil, maintaining a correspondence with her to this day; and how she had returned home at the age of seventeen, quite innocent of the ways of the world; yet this very unworldliness gave her a particular charm, her mother continued, warming increasingly to her theme. At any rate, since her daughter had once more been dwelling there, her hitherto tranquil house was visited far more frequently by their neighbours. So foolish were some of the young caballeros, and even some of the older ones, in their pursuit of her daughter, that she, as a mother, felt cause for concern. Yet she knew well her child's chaste mind and her pure character. The life of the cloister still held a deep attraction for her, and no man had yet been able to offer her a more attractive alternative. In the meantime Doña Clara expressed the hope of placing her in the Aljafería in the coming winter, where the previous year she had already been introduced to the Infanta Maria. There, she said, her daughter would meet men of a different quality from those she was meeting in this provincial backwater. If one of them did not succeed in winning Leonor's heart, she would be greatly surprised.

Thus spoke Doña Clara, as she continued to refill their glasses with the delicious liqueur. Even her son felt embarrassed at how thickly she was laying it on, and several times he tried to interrupt her. Yet Don Nuño allowed her to talk on and on, even encouraging her with further questions, secretly astonished at himself, as he listened intently to the outpourings of this matchmaking woman, which only the day before he had found so repellent. Yet, how pleasant it was, here on the terrace, sipping their liqueurs, whilst all around them the trees seemed to be rustling mysteriously in the soft breeze of the evening, with the chirping of the cicadas and a myriad of stars shining down from the vast firmament...

They sat together until well after midnight, and when at last they retired to bed Don Nuño was still unable to sleep. Filled with a strange sense of unrest, he stood at the open window of his chamber, staring out at the clear, starry night. Suddenly he gave a start. Was that not a shadow flitting through the grounds? Now he thought he could hear the faint sound of footsteps. Or was it merely the sound of the wind rustling in the trees? He listened intently, straining his eyes to see in the darkness, yet all was still. What could it have been? A servant girl keeping a tryst with her lover in the grounds? Or could it be that Doña Leonor was not as pure and chaste as her scheming mother believed...?

This very thought pierced Don Nuño like a stab to the heart and once again he felt astonishment at himself. Was he jealous, he, a de Luna? Jealous of a girl whom he had only known for a day, who was socially far beneath him? Shrugging his shoulders, he turned away from the window and went to bed.

V

He woke late the following morning. His head was aching from the large amount of liqueur he had drunk the previous evening, and he could not rid himself of that strange sense of unrest. At breakfast he was silent, his expression almost grim. Again and again his glance strayed towards Doña Leonor who sat opposite him at the table. She calmly carried on with her meal; yet he thought he could glimpse that hidden gleam behind her lowered lids, just as in the church, when he had espied this far away look, and again he would gladly have known what passion, what dark secret lay hidden within her charming frame.

Her guest's state of mind did not escape the sharp eyes of Doña Clara, but she merely perceived that which could benefit her design. When breakfast was over she quite shamelessly suggested to her daughter that she accompany the Count on a stroll through the grounds which contained some plants and old trees that were well worth seeing. Her Leonor would surely be glad to show them to their dear guest, wouldn't she?

Her mother's quite blatant request broke abruptly into Doña Leonor's dreamy reverie. Blushing deeply, she gazed first at her mother and then at the Count; but before she could raise any objection, Doña Clara and her son left the room under the pretext of having to make certain arrangements for their guest. Meanwhile the Count gallantly made haste to offer Doña Leonor his arm, so that she had no choice but to obey her mother and accompany him into the grounds.

Don Nuño's heart beat faster as he found himself alone at her side for the first time. He was well practised in conversing with ladies, but now he could think of nothing to say beyond uttering a few stiff compliments about the spaciousness of the grounds and the beautiful flowers. Doña Leonor answered automatically; but hardly had they left the main pathway leading through the grounds, where they could be seen from the house, and turned onto a narrower path, lined with bushes, when she suddenly came to a halt, abruptly withdrew her arm from his, and looked up at him with a look of pained determination.

'I must confess something to you, Count', she began, sharply interrupting his attempt to speak. 'I would be giving you poor thanks for your kindness if I were not to make clear to you what they are planning. My mother did not send us off together in order that I might show you the plants. It is rather that she is hoping… that she is trying…You are surely too noble, Count, to mock us. Well, in short, my mother is trying to find a husband for me – a rich husband, if you understand…'

Perhaps I would not be adverse, Don Nuño was about to respond with a gallant, joking reply; but he was affected by her embarrassment, and the frivolous tone died on his lips.

'You are not the first to have been invited here for this reason', Doña Leonor continued sorrowfully. 'But do not think badly of us because of this. My mother and my brother are worthy people –

it is only our poverty that drives them to such… Forgive me, I find it hard… It will be better if I leave you now.'

And before he had the chance to prevent her, she, blushing more deeply than ever, took the next path and disappeared into the park, whilst he remained standing for a long time, rooted to the spot. Without a shadow of a doubt she had spoken from the heart, from the purest of motives; but if she had been the most calculating of cocottes she could not have devised a better means of fascinating Don Nuño than with this scene. The very fact that she clearly was not in the least interested in gaining his admiration only served to increase it.

For the afternoon Doña Clara had invited guests from the neighbourhood, and in the evening there was even dancing. On this occasion Don Nuño once more noted with irritation how desperately the lady of the house tried to cling to the façade of a lifestyle which long since been beyond her means. The wine was of inferior quality, clearly watered down, but served in elegant carafes; and the music was provided by two old men, presumably peasants from the village, whom Doña Clara had dressed absurdly in servants' livery. How the noise of their fiddle-playing grated on Don Nuño's nerves! How the insipid red wine disgusted him, although he drank one glass after another! Into what kind of society had he fallen? With ill humour he watched as Doña Leonor danced with different young gentlemen, yet she did not seem to be on intimate terms with any of the visitors. In this respect at least the old woman had been right: the country bumpkins from the immediate vicinity posed no danger to this girl. But what if Doña Clara continued to invite gentlemen of rank to her house? Or if she really were to establish her daughter in the Aljafería? A girl of such beauty would surely attract admirers there, who would not care about her humble background – who would stop at nothing…

At this thought Don Nuño felt a stab to the heart, and the realisation came to him: this must never happen. None other than he should be permitted to call this precious creature his own. However unexpected this was to himself, how little it corresponded to the life he had planned, it was she, Doña Leonor de Sesé, the little girl from the provinces, of lower nobility, she was the one he had chosen, the one who would live by his side in the Castillo in A.

Although he felt bitter resentment at being obliged to fall in with the de Sesé's matchmaking designs, he determined to speak to the family at the earliest opportunity, as their agreement would establish his position as the rightful bridegroom. That very evening, after the guests had departed, and Doña Leonor had withdrawn to her room, in the abrupt fashion that was her wont, the Count, who wished to put this humiliating conversation behind him as soon as possible, sought out the mother and brother in order to acquaint them with his wishes. Doña Clara could hardly contain her glee: her daughter to be Countess de Luna! Don Guillén, whose prospects in the army could only benefit from such a brother in law, also expressed his deep satisfaction at how things had developed. Once again they sat together until after midnight, drinking wine and liqueurs and toasting the future happiness of the two houses, now to be linked. They even began discussing the best time for the wedding celebrations to take place.

There was just one question upon which not one word passed their lips, namely how Doña Leonor would react to the idea of the marriage that had been decided upon; yet each of the three entertained secret apprehensions on that score. It was only too obvious that there were problems to be expected. Doña Leonor had not given the Count the slightest encouragement. She appeared not to think of him as a possible admirer, or bridegroom at all, and she certainly was not the kind of girl who would submit to being married off by her family without her consent. But Don Nuño set his hopes on her not being blind to the honour he was doing her, by choosing her as his bride, and also on the fact that, as he knew quite well, he was not lacking in qualities and means that might win a woman's affections. One day she would be his, in body and soul, and the king himself would envy him the possession of such a wife.

After they had finally separated and retired for the night, the Count stood for a long time at the open window of his bedchamber, his mind filled with these pleasurable thoughts. Yet this very position served as a reminder of the precarious nature of his happiness, for it recalled to his mind that strange shadow which he had observed from the window the previous night, and of the suspicion which had then arisen in his heart. He had almost forgotten this sensation due to the eventfulness of the day – almost, but not totally. It had remained at the back of his mind the whole time, a vague sense of apprehension that weighed on his emotions. And now, as he once more stood at the window, gazing out at the moonlit night, he felt this sense of apprehension grow stronger, until it finally took total possession of him. There seemed to be something in the air, and he found it impossible to move from the spot before he had discovered what it was.

He must have stood there for over an hour, with nothing to hear but the sounds of the cicadas. But all of a sudden, just when his tiredness was threatening to overcome his suspense, he gave a start, aware that something was happening outside. He looked up and was just in time to catch a glimpse of a figure clad in white, crossing the main pathway at the back of the grounds and disappearing behind the high bushes of the park.

Swiftly, he threw a cloak over his shoulders, buckled on his sword, and swung himself over the balustrade. His bedchamber was situated on the first floor, but he was able to climb down easily by clinging to the vine-covered trellis, and hastened, as if pursued by furies, along the main path into the darkness of the grounds. His glimpse of the figure which he was following had been almost as fleeting as it had been the previous night. It could be an errant maidservant, or a figment of his own overstretched imagination. But instinct told him that it was no maid and certainly no figment of his imagination. He had only to think of Doña Leonor, as she sat at the breakfast table, seemingly lost in a dream, yet with shining eyes, to be certain that the errant figure in the grounds was none other than – his bride!

Now he found himself approximately at the spot where he had seen the figure dive into the bushes. Cautiously he took the next path that led in the same direction. The moon was shedding sufficient light, but there was nothing to be seen. For a while he wandered, crisscrossing the narrow paths through the grounds, searching in vain for the figure. Yet when he was beginning to despair of finding her, he suddenly espied a flickering light. He hastened thither and found himself in a clearing where there was a small wooden house, a white garden pavilion, designed to offer a delightful place for repose during the day, yet which at night, in the pale moonlight, assumed a deserted, almost sinister aspect.

At once Don Nuño saw that he had reached his nocturnal goal. A burning lantern had been placed on the side wall of the pavilion and behind it he caught sight of the white clad figure. He took two, three quiet paces, darting into the shadow of the pavilion, and inched his way along its wall until he was able to shelter behind a large vine. Cautiously he pushed aside the vine leaves, and there – his heart almost stopped – he espied, as large as life, the sight that had at first aroused his suspicion, but which nonetheless struck him now like a thunderbolt: on the steps of the pavilion stood Doña Leonor, attired in a white gown and eagerly awaiting someone.

The shock of the moment was so great that Don Nuño was unable to restrain himself. He drew breath and made to draw his sword as if he were about to run the girl through. Hearing the sound, Doña Leonor swiftly turned towards it. 'Manrique?' she whispered in a soft and tender voice.

Don Nuño, his hand still on the sword and totally incapable of rational thought, stepped boldly out from behind the shadow of the vine. But whereas he was able to recognise her face quite clearly in the light of the lantern, she could only barely make out the outline of his; and before he was able to utter a word, she cried out full of joy: 'Manrique!', hurried towards him and impetuously cast her arms around his neck.

The Count was thrown totally off balance by this unexpected turn of events. He had wanted to confront her angrily, to berate her, to curse her. But now, as he felt her slender body nestling against his, with such abandon, all the harsh words that were on his lips, died away. He lost his senses and was seized by the insane temptation to carry on playing the role of his unknown rival, on and on to the ultimate moment of bliss! Already he was drawing his beloved closer, his hands, trembling with desire, was exploring her enchanting body, and who knows what he might have been tempted to do, had not at that very moment a sound penetrated the night, a strange sound that was totally unexpected in such a place. A singing was heard, the soft singing of a male voice, intoning the melody of a popular Andalusian love song: 'Time and space were lost to me, I saw you in eternity' – just this one line, like a signal. The bushes in front of the pavilion parted and a man emerged into the clearing. Like Don Nuño he wore a cloak, was of roughly the same build and height, so the girl's mistake was understandable. Yet the face that was now visible in the light of the lantern, a young, open face with dark eyes and noble features, was totally unknown to the Count, although it did remind him faintly of someone.

Doña Leonor had turned in horror, but one of her delicate arms was still resting lightly on Don Nuño's shoulder, as she stared in sheer amazement at the sudden apparition. The two men were also confused. The Count, as he looked at the stranger, felt a mingled sensation of embarrassment and wrath; what then must have been the feelings of Doña Leonor's secret lover, at finding her at their meeting place so unexpectedly in the company, indeed in the arms of another man! The smile of expectant joy faded from his face as he stepped closer, hesitating, and uncertain whether his eyes were deceiving him – and then Doña Leonor recognized him, and with a second glance she also recognized the man whom she was embracing. She uttered a cry of shock, tore her arm from Don Nuño's shoulder, as if from a poisonous viper, and dashed towards the other man, clinging to his shoulder as if taking refuge there.

'Manrique!' she cried, looking at Don Nuño with an expression of revulsion and horror. 'For the love of God, he must have followed me here! He was suddenly standing there in front of me, I thought it was you…!'

'But – you know this man?' Manrique asked in astonishment.

'It is the Count de Luna, a friend of my brother's', Doña Leonor explained. 'He is spending the holiday with us.'

'The Count de Luna', repeated Manrique with a frown, and in a tone which suggested that this name meant something to him. But Don Nuño did not allow him time to consider.

'Yes, the Count de Luna!' he exclaimed in fury, as he strode towards the surprised pair. 'A friend of the family and as such I have the right to defend their honour! But who are you, you damned villain, and what are you doing at this hour trespassing on the estate of the de Sesé family?'

Doña Leonor trembled and hid her face against Manrique's shoulder. He, however seemed to reflect on how to deflect this harsh rebuke.

'My name is Manrique Corda' he declared at last, clearly attempting to moderate the tone of the exchange. 'And Doña Leonor is my betrothed.'

'Ah, your betrothed!' Don Nuño exclaimed mockingly. 'The family will no doubt be delighted to hear this!'

At this point he would have been only too glad to declare whose betrothed Doña Leonor really was, but here he was unfortunately obliged to keep silent. If this upstart nobody – for he surely could not be a gentleman – enjoyed Doña Leonor's favour without the knowledge of her family, Don Nuño was placed in a similarly awkward position, only in reverse, having the family's blessing as the rightful bridegroom, but without the knowledge of the bride.

It was Doña Leonor who finally found words to express this situation. Until now she had been too shocked and horrified by the Count's appearance on the scene to have considered the presumption of his manner; but now it began to anger her. She threw back her head and spoke with a haughty, if not completely steady, voice: 'May I ask, Count, what business is this of yours? By what right do you persecute me and meddle in the affairs of my family?'

'You would do better to be silent!' cried Don Nuño in a rage, with the embittered tone of a deceived husband. 'A fine lady you are, who plays the innocent by day and at night creeps out to meet her paramour in the grounds! You deserve to be shut away in a cloister for the rest of your life!'

'How dare you?' cried Manrique, who was far more enraged by the insults hurled at Doña Leonor than by those aimed at him. 'You will give me satisfaction for this! If you do not offer your apology to the lady forthwith...'

'The devil take you!' snarled the Count in fury. 'I will teach you to drag a girl from a good family down into the dirt! You shall forfeit to me your life for the disgrace you have brought upon this family!'

Doña Leonor uttered a shriek and desperately implored the two men to desist, but they had both already drawn their swords and were furiously attacking each other.

Meanwhile there were signs of activity in the grounds: presumably alarmed by the sounds of the struggle, some servants advanced along the main pathway towards the clearing, bearing pitchforks and lanterns. Doña Leonor saw them coming and called out an anxious warning, but the men, grimly locked in battle, only desisted when the glimmer of the lanterns actually fell upon the pavilion.

Wringing her hands, Doña Leonor begged Manrique to flee for his life. But he still hesitated, unwilling to abandon her to the other man. The Count too was undecided as to what to do. Should he behave as the defender of the family and shout out directions to the servants, demanding that the audacious interloper be apprehended? But would he not then be risking the exposure of Doña Leonor? And how was he to explain his own presence there?

Meanwhile Manrique had decided to appeal to the Count's sense of honour. 'I beseech you', he spoke softly and rapidly, 'if you really care for the good name of this lady, do not expose it to the mockery of the servants!' And without waiting for an answer, he pressed Doña Leonor's hand and vanished into the bushes.

There was no more time to be lost – the steps and voices had already come dangerously close to the clearing. The Count stepped towards Doña Leonor and grasped her arm firmly, intending to lead her away with him; but in fury she tore herself from his grasp, and hastened away along the darkest path. He saw her white dress shimmering through the trees, yet when he hurried after her she vanished, as if swallowed up by the undergrowth. He wandered about the grounds for a long time afterwards, hiding from the servants, who believed him to be the interloper, so that in the end he was fortunate to be able to regain entry into the house unseen.

VII

For the rest of the night there could be no thought of sleep. Tormented by dreadful images, Don Nuño tossed and turned on his bed. His reason demanded that he put an immediate end to the whole vexatious story. Without further ado he could explain to the de Sesés that Doña Leonor was unworthy to be the Countess de Luna; he could depart from thence, free and unencumbered, and then seek a more suitable wife. But this simple possibility could not have been further from Don Nuño's mind. Indeed, his passionate desire to possess Doña Leonor had only been intensified by the scene in the grounds. He had merely to picture her to himself, as she stood in the clearing, a white clad figure, her expectant face transfigured by love, and every thought of giving her up and parting from her, vanished entirely. In that one brief moment, when she flung her arms round his neck, heaven had opened up to him – and then the other man had come. Don Nuño ground his teeth. Who was that? How had he succeeded in becoming intimate with Doña Leonor? This man had no right to live! No man had the right to live, if he came between him, de Luna, and his chosen bride!

By the time morning came he had devised a plan as to what action he should take and he sank finally into a restless slumber. When he awoke and went down to breakfast the sun was already high in the sky. On the terrace he encountered, in addition to Don Guillén and Doña Clara, the steward of the estate, who was giving them a deferential account of an incident that had occurred in the night. It was apparent that a few drunken fellows had managed to gain access to the grounds, had argued loudly and kicked up a racket. Indeed they had broken a few branches and trampled down a few plants, but thankfully the damage was not extensive. Unfortunately the servants had not been able to apprehend the troublemakers in the darkness.

The owners of the estate paid little heed to these tidings, being inwardly preoccupied with more important matters. Early in the morning Doña Clara had visited her daughter's bedchamber in order to acquaint her with the magnificent offer of marriage made to her by the Count de Luna. However, the result of this conversation surpassed her worst expectations. Doña Leonor had rejected the proposal point blank, in a most resolute manner; indeed at the very idea she had almost fallen into a fit of hysterics. She did not wish even to set eyes on the Count, having learned of his desire. In fact she had refused to leave her bedchamber until the two gentlemen had departed. Her only hope was that the Count might have changed his mind overnight. Doña Clara was perplexed as to why the girl should come by such a thought. She felt not inconsiderable embarrassment when she encountered her daughter's suitor. But to her astonishment Don Nuño showed no surprise. Impatiently he waved aside her wordy explanations of her daughter's behaviour and he himself began to speak in a resolute tone.

He declared that he deeply regretted having begun his courtship in such unfavourable circumstances, but was confident of being able to bring it to a favourable conclusion in the future. He would stand by his claim of which he had been certain as a result of the family's agreement only the day before; yet if Doña Leonor needed time to become familiar with the new situation, he thought it unwise to put pressure on her. He would leave the house that very day, he assured her, for he had in any case certain affairs to attend to in Zaragoza before his vacation was at an end. He had but one request, and that was to be permitted to write a few lines to his intended.

The de Sesés attempted to persuade him to remain, but they were soon obliged to admit that his departure would not be so bad an idea in the present difficult circumstances. The Count's visit had borne fruit, as it had been hoped that it would, and to achieve a successful outcome, that of changing the girl's mind, his presence was not needed, indeed it might possibly prove to be an obstacle. As soon as mass had been said, Don Nuño bade the servants pack his bags and, taking up his quill, he penned a few lines to Doña Leonor. He declared that he was determined to do all in his power to call her his own. He would brook no refusal, would tolerate no rival. It was a fiery love letter, but the tone was darkly threatening, more likely to alarm a woman than to stir her affection. He was himself aware of this, yet he did not wish to change anything. So he sealed the letter and had it sent immediately to Doña Leonor's bedchamber.

There was one more delicate matter to be arranged before he could leave the house: he must see to it that the nocturnal meetings between Doña Leonor and Manrique be terminated, once and for all. He must make sure of this, whilst taking care not to reveal the girl's secret.

After their parting meal he took Doña Clara aside and explained to her with an air of authority, as the new head of the family, that his future bride should be provided with stronger protection than had hitherto been the case when the girl had been unattached. From now on certain precautions were essential; for instance, the door to Doña Leonor's chamber should be locked at night, her correspondence should be checked, and any servants with whom she appeared to be over familiar should be removed. Also, an incident such as that which had taken place the previous night in the grounds, made it necessary that a strong guard be installed. He would be happy to bear any extra costs that these measures should entail. Nothing was more precious to him than the safety and welfare of the future Countess de Luna.

Naturally, his intention to bring an end to the nightly meetings in the grounds, but at the same time also to conceal his knowledge of them could only be met with limited success. He had expected no less, nor deep down would he have wished it. True, her mother assured him at great length that Doña Leonor's virtue was beyond all reproach and therefore did not need guarding over. But it was clear to him that her suspicions had been aroused – presumably by the vehemence with which the girl had rejected the marriage proposal. Doña Clara would keep a strict watch over her daughter, of that the Count could be certain; and for the rest he was confident that there would soon be nobody from whom she needed to be guarded.

He was in good spirits as he prepared to take leave of his hosts and was about to swing himself into the saddle when Doña Leonor's chambermaid came running out of the house and handed him a note from her mistress. It was a response to the letter that he had sent her, which had clearly caused her deep distress. She wrote that his words had 'made her tremble', and she implored the Count beseechingly to desist from his courtship.

You know full well, Count, or you should know, that I can never be yours – that my heart belongs to another. Last night, when you, a total stranger, penetrated my secret, I felt it to be a disaster, but now I will call it a blessing, if it should persuade you to give up your intention. The bad opinion, which in your own words you now have of me, will make this decision easier for you. You surely cannot love a woman if she does not hold your respect. And you cannot believe in all earnestness that you could find happiness with a woman if you kill the man she loves. What you write to me in this regard has made my blood run cold, but I will ascribe it to your state of mind in the heat of the moment. If you leave this house and never enter it again, I will still retain a feeling of kindness and respect towards you. But if you persist in your desire, then I fear that it will destroy both of us.

In fury the Count crumpled the letter in his hand. Don Guillén and Doña Clara, who had come out of the house to take leave of him, exchanged anxious looks. This matter of arranging a marriage was proving a far more difficult affair than they had ever envisaged. However, Don Nuño had swiftly gained control of himself and thrust the crumpled letter into his pocket. He mounted his horse, briefly made his farewells once more and galloped away.

Part Two
Son from Afar

I

The very same evening the Count arrived in Zaragoza, he sought out an old acquaintance, Lieutenant Gomez, in order to ask him to find out all he could concerning Manrique Corda. He was aware that it would be no easy task to gather information about a man of whom nothing was known but his name, and he believed the lieutenant, a shrewd and devious old campaigner, to be the right man for the task. He moved in many circles, knew everything about everything, and was little troubled by scruples if his intuition told him that there was a prospect of a rich reward.

But to Don Nuño's surprise there was no need to invoke his intuition, as Lieutenant Gomez already knew all about the man. 'How comes it' he asked in amazement, 'that you wish to learn something of Manrique Corda? Well, that does not require much effort on my part, glad as I would be of your money, Count. Anyone in this town can tell you who Manrique Corda is – he is not lacking in popularity.' And then he related to his eager listener how this had come about.

Once a year the arena of Zaragoza served as the scene of a great singing tournament whose origins went far back to the glorious old times of the troubadours and minstrels. Every singer worth his salt came from far and wide to participate, for to win it was held to be a great honour. It was the custom however, to permit anyone who deemed himself endowed with a good singing voice to enter the competition; thus it was not uncommon to see total strangers in the throng of singers, mingling with familiar faces. Appearing alongside the first tenors of the court were also to be seen ragged street entertainers who usually performed their songs in the alleyways and public houses, seeking to gain favour with the ladies or at least to be rewarded with a good dinner. Young officers made their appearance there, bellowing out robust martial songs, alongside slender sons of noblemen singing their own romantic lyrics. They all had to face the rigorous scrutiny of the Zaragoza people, an expert and highly critical audience, who not infrequently expressed themselves in a chorus of shrill whistles, or even by throwing rotten eggs and tomatoes. But as harsh as this public could be in its condemnation, it could be equally generous in its praise, regardless of the singer's rank, and more than once it had caused a totally unknown singer to triumph over the great and the famous.

The previous year, the day of the competition had happened to fall on the birthday of the Castilian Infanta Maria, whose family had only shortly before taken up residence in the Aljafería, after Fernando had been awarded the crown. A natural consequence of this was that the Infanta became the patroness of the singing tournament. She sat amongst her ladies on a raised seat in the royal box, and if she looked graciously upon a singer, he at once pictured himself wearing the crown of victory.

The great Berlini, who was generally expected to win the competition, as he was known to be the Infanta's favourite singer, had just performed a most intricate and difficult aria; all were filled with admiration, and there was little doubt in anyone's mind that he would be the victor. But next came the turn of a young singer whom no one in Zaragoza had ever seen before. He was plainly dressed, and appeared almost diffident, as if he were not accustomed to perform before such a multitude. Yet no sooner had he begun to sing than the public were held in thrall. He sang, accompanying himself on the lute, a bitter-sweet ballad about a doomed love, with such a strange, peculiar melody, as if from far away shores; yet he sang in their native tongue and his graceful delivery gave the impression that he had been well taught, although he had none of the artificial virtuosity displayed by such as Berlini. But what mostly stirred the hearts of his listeners, the female ones in particular, was not so much the voice itself, which, if truth be told, was somewhat lacking in power, but rather the deeply felt emotion that the young singer conveyed.

When he came to the end of his song thunderous applause broke out. The spectators leapt from their seats, with shouts of 'bravo' and a storm of clapping. The ladies in particular went wild, and when the competition came to an end, it was they who raised the tumultuous cry that victory should go to the young stranger, and to no other.

There was only one lady who totally disagreed with this judgement, and it was her vote that carried the most weight: the Infanta Maria, patroness of the singing tournament, insisted on awarding the laurel wreath to Berlini, and refused to countenance the idea that an unknown stranger of low degree should have beaten her favourite. It was a conflict between the will of the people and that of the ruler. At first the Master of Ceremonies, wishing to please the Infanta, declared Berlini to be the winner of the contest, but this provoked such a storm of protest from the public that he was forced to revoke his decision. He regretfully explained to Doña Maria that in accordance with ancient tradition the tournament was to be judged along strictly democratic principles, and to the resounding cheers of the crowd, declared Manrique Corda – as the stranger called himself – to be definitely and incontrovertibly the winner. But now the Infanta, enraged by her defeat, refused to set the laurel wreath on his brow, as the First Lady of the Court must do. For some considerable time the winner had been standing there, waiting to be thus honoured, the spectators were beginning to murmur threateningly, and the Master of Ceremonies nervously began to urge Doña Maria to comply with the people's wish; but she hissed that it was a scandal, an affront against her person as well as against her father's royal dignity, and with bitter tears in her eyes she swore that she would never lower herself so far as to condone the affront, in her own court and on her birthday.

At this awkward moment something extraordinary took place: one of the court ladies sitting close by the Infanta arose from her seat, took up the laurel wreath and before anyone could prevent her, stepped up to the front of the balustrade. The victor understood and likewise stepped forward, sank down upon one knee before her and looked up at the young lady in astonishment and manifest admiration. Indeed she was a delight to behold: a maiden, delicate as a flower in bud, clad in a white gown, with glorious shining hair and solemn, almond-shaped eyes. A whispering went through the crowd at her appearance that grew into tumultuous applause as she ceremoniously placed the laurel wreath upon his head. Manrique Corda seized her hand and pressed it to his lips with a fiery look; she, however, blushing deeply and suddenly bereft of the boldness with which she had acted until then, tore her hand away as if it had been burned, and hastily resumed her place. The applause continued unabated, and the Infanta turned pale with fury.

But then the Master of Ceremonies called for silence, as the conclusion of the festival required the winner to sing a special song in honour of the Infanta, the patroness of the festival. Manrique Corda chose to sing an ancient Andalusian romantic ballad: 'Time and space were lost to me, I saw you in eternity'. He sang with passionate intensity but his gaze was directed not at the Infanta but at the lady of the court who had presented him with the laurel wreath.

Thus had ended the singing championship of the previous year, and it had remained the subject of Zaragoza's gossip for many weeks afterwards. Of course, it was the mystery surrounding the person of the victor that so aroused people's emotions. There were rumours that he was an escaped prisoner, a gipsy who camped in the woods with his fellow robbers and cut people's throats. Others swore blindly that he was a prince from a noble family who was travelling incognito through the country. The rumours were further strengthened by the fact that when the championship had ended, he had declined all invitations and had disappeared the very same evening, God knows where – but not before he had made pressing enquiries to the Master of Ceremonies concerning the lady who had presented him with the laurel wreath.

This provided a further target for public curiosity, for it seemed obvious to surmise that here was the beginning of a romantic love story. Fortunately it was possible to find out more about the heroine of the story than about her admirer. Born in T. into the lower ranks of the nobility, she had only recently arrived in the city, accompanied by her ambitious mother, and had been presented at court. There, on account of her beauty and apparently modest conduct, she had immediately found favour and had been given a position among the Infanta's court ladies. She had already been graciously offered the prospect of spending the entire season at court, and perhaps even the winter in the Aljafería – as is well known, princes like to adorn their courts with beautiful young people – but after the scandal at the singing tournament, Doña Maria's graciousness had withered. She called the mother of the rebellious girl to her and informed her frostily that her daughter's presence was no longer required. There was no need for an additional lady in waiting at the present time. She could try her luck with the girl again the following summer, if she had by then managed to instruct her on how to conduct herself in a seemly manner.

Thereupon the young lady and her mother had departed, greatly to the regret of the citizens of Zaragoza, who were full of sympathy for her. As she climbed into the carriage her face was covered in a heavy veil and no one could tell what was going on in her heart. But all were convinced that she would be pining away day and night for the singer on account of whom she had incurred the disfavour of the Infanta, and they wondered whether this romance might have a future, or whether it was doomed.

This, however, remained a mystery to the good burghers, and so eventually the whole affair began to fade from their minds, due to the lack of any new information that might feed the gossip – until, only a few weeks ago, it had unexpectedly gained fresh impetus. One of the king's ministers had gone into the camp of the rebel Count d'Urgell in order to conduct negotiations, and had happened to observe amongst his followers none other than Manrique Corda, whom he still remembered well. The minister, astonished at finding the sensitive singer in so warlike an environment, had made enquiries concerning him and had learned that Manrique Corda had been fighting in d'Urgell's service for more than a year. Despite the fact that he appeared to be of lowly or unverifiable origin, he had advanced to the rank of a captain and had, by all accounts, excelled himself on several occasions. It seemed that he enjoyed the confidence, indeed, the personal friendship of d'Urgell, and should the Count succeed in winning the crown, it was likely that he would help the singer to achieve a brilliant future at court.

This revelation provoked a scandal in the Aljafería. The Infanta was incensed; her innermost feelings had been outraged at the idea that a rebel, an enemy of the crown, should have the temerity to come to Zaragoza – to take part in 'her' singing tournament! How had it been possible that he had actually been selected as the winner! Her instinct had been quite correct when she had resisted the choice of the populace! But there would not be such a choice at the next singing competition! New rules would be introduced! From now on the victor would be selected by acknowledged experts, not by the ignorant masses! And before the tournament took place, the background and respectability of each competitor would be stringently examined!

The music loving burghers of Zaragoza received these directives with audible displeasure. It was the very openness and spontaneity of the event that had always created the particular charm of the singing tournament. Once more a piece of tradition was to be broken, a tradition that had originated in those glorious times when the art of song was not the sole preserve of princes, but had its source deep in the hearts of the common people. Now it would be the Berlinis who always would win and the troubadours would be relegated to the gutter.

Yet in no way did Manrique Corda's popularity suffer on account of this revelation – on the contrary, his appearance on the scene was seen as a bold act of bravado, for which he was all the more admired. There was much belated laughter at the memory of his audacity in appearing before the royal family, and it was deeply regretted that there was little likelihood of his voice being heard again within the walls of Zaragoza. In the fullness of time, this topic of conversation would naturally have been exhausted, but now it had practically grown into a local legend, which was embellished in countless variations as it went from mouth to mouth.

II

Thus far went Lieutenant Gomez' account, to which, as might be imagined, the Count de Luna listened with wrapt attention. Various details which had hitherto puzzled him were now explained – for example, Doña Leonor's lively interest in the civil war, and her mother's somewhat vague story of their visit to Zaragoza. The old woman had been so garrulous, yet had totally forgotten to mention that her paragon of a daughter had fallen out of favour with the Infanta. Well, this could be rectified, and Don Nuño was the man to do so. He had determined upon this even before the Lieutenant had ended his story.

As far as Manrique was concerned, this now confirmed the Count's previous assumption, that the man lacked the rank to count in any way as a serious rival to the planned marriage. Even if there had been no other suitor, the de Sesé family would never have agreed to a marriage linking their daughter and an unknown troubadour of dubious origins. Furthermore, the fact that he was an enemy of the rightful ruler, meant that in the context of the civil war he could be considered an outlaw. If someone were to remove him from the scene he would not meet with any unpleasantness, as would be the case in times of peace: on the contrary, he would be doing a good deed and would be rendering a service to the crown.

His curiosity far from satisfied, the Count now explained to the Lieutenant that he wished to learn everything that was known in Zaragoza concerning Manrique Corda. Where had he come from so suddenly? Where had he learned to sing? Did he have family, and if so, where did they live? Where was he himself staying at present? Every detail could be of consequence! Don Nuño impressed this upon the Lieutenant and asked to be kept constantly informed. He encouraged the man's eagerness with a few ducats, and held out the prospect of many more if he worked well, taking his leave of him with the sense that he had made considerable progress.

The next morning saw him passing through the gateway of the Aljafería, where he sought a private audience with the Infanta Maria. He was not acquainted with the lady, other than exchanging a few polite words at balls and court receptions. But now he addressed her as he would a sister and confided to her in deferential terms that he had recently become engaged to Leonor de Sesé. Leonor de Sesé? The name reminded Doña Maria of something, and Don Nuño was only too willing to jog her memory. Did she recall the singing tournament – the young girl who had crowned the victor, a certain Manrique Corda?

The Infanta immediately pricked up her ears. It was exactly as Don Nuño had hoped. She had not forgotten her grievance, neither towards Manrique Corda, nor towards Doña Leonor. Unfortunately, the Count went on to relate, that encounter between the two seemed to have been not the only one, and this had led to a certain reluctance on her part. Regrettably, he, Don Nuño, was obliged to return to the front the very next morning, leaving her in the care of her foolish mother. How comforted he would be if he knew his bride to be in an environment where she would be protected from dangerous influences and prepared for her future role as Countess de Luna.

God alone knows what Doña Maria made of Don Nuño's story, but the upshot was that within a little more than an hour's audience with her he had achieved more than Doña Clara had in weeks. The Infanta assented to taking Doña Leonor back to her court – assented even with alacrity, with a barely suppressed smile of triumph, as Don Nuño noted to his satisfaction. Although he did not specifically intend to torment Doña Leonor, he did consider that her conduct demanded a certain degree of retribution.

But above all he wished her to be kept under strict observation and he believed the Infanta to be just the right person for that task.

Only a few days later the De Sesé family received a letter informing them of the honour that was to be bestowed on Doña Leonor. This provoked dramatic scenes. Doña Leonor did not want to be a lady of the court. She remembered with a shudder the icy look with which the Infanta had dismissed her, and it was easy to guess that none other than the Count de Luna was behind her unexpected reinstatement. She desperately implored her mother not to take her back to Zaragoza, but Doña Clara was understandably in no mood to accede to this wish. Not only did this run counter to her maternal ambition but she was also motivated by a certain suspicion which had been aroused by the Count's final instructions to her. Further more, it would have been difficult for even the most indulgent of mothers to disobey the Infanta of Castile and Aragon.

Thus within a short time mother and daughter found themselves once more within the walls of the Aljafería. At the first audience Doña Leonor made a disagreeable impression. When the Infanta welcomed her with the words 'Ah, the bride of Count de Luna!' she contradicted the Infanta, answering heatedly that she had declined the Count's offer, and that she had no intention of changing her mind. Doña Maria attempted to cover the foolish outburst with an indulgent smile, but Doña Clara was greatly dismayed. She regarded with horror what she perceived as persistent stubbornness on the part of Doña Leonor, but she also observed the dislike, indeed, hatred that was concealed beneath the dignified manner of the princess.

She had hoped to be able to spend a few weeks with her daughter, but Doña Maria was of the opinion that this would not be in accordance with the Count's wishes and she politely made it abundantly clear that the mother should return home without delay. Once more Doña Clara had no alternative but to submit, although her sense of unease had now grown almost stronger than her feeling of pride at the honour bestowed on her daughter. She was unable to believe that the Infanta's influence would work in favour of the Count's purpose – she knew her daughter too well for that. So she decided that before leaving she would write to the Abbess of the convent where Doña Leonor had been educated. The convent was situated not far from the gates of the city, and thus easily reached for occasional visits. The Abbess was an excellent person, highly regarded by the young girl, and her influence would surely hold some sway over her.

So Doña Clara explained in deferential words to the Abbess that her daughter had through the grace of God attracted a suitor who would be the dream of any woman. She painted a portrait of the Count in the warmest and most glowing of colours: he had riches and an elegant life style, he was handsome, well educated and pious – all these qualities and more were compounded in this rare man. But the most important thing of all was, that he loved Leonor deeply, he was willing to lay down his life for her, and would make her one of the first ladies in the realm.

But, the mother continued, the girl was refusing to accept him, be it out of defiance, overwrought nerves, or a foolish emotional confusion – who could divine what lay in a young girl's heart? Her own mother would be the last to know. She wished only to prevent Leonor from missing this great chance of happiness, because of a momentary whim that she would soon overcome and later regret. Unfortunately, she continued, she was at present unable to prevail upon the girls feelings with wise advice and loving words. Therefore she was humbly requesting the Abbess to use her influence with the girl and help her find the right path from which she had strayed.

Doña Clara sent this message to the Abbess shortly before she was due to return to her estate. Doña Leonor wept bitterly when she had to part from her mother. Now she felt totally alone and a stranger in this world of riches and exotic entertainments, without a kindred soul to commune with. The Infanta took much delight in introducing her everywhere as 'the Count de Luna's betrothed', and was skilled at tormenting her in different, subtle ways, while the ladies of the court, well aware that Doña Maria did not like the girl, treated her with disdain and avoided her company.

Such was the situation of the girl when she received an unexpected letter from the Abbess. The old lady had herself received Doña Clara's letter, which had caused her some consternation. She had corresponded with her former pupil from time to time, but had been given no intimation of the matter about which Doña Clara had written to her. All that Doña Leonor had reported to her was that she was living in Zaragoza now as a lady of the court, and so the Abbess answered accordingly. Without mentioning her mother's message, she warmly invited her pupil to pay her a visit. She could surely ask the Infanta for a day's leave from her duties and with a good carriage the convent was in easy reach.

It can be imagined with what joy Doña Leonor read this letter and accepted the invitation at a time when she so longed for some affection and human warmth. She went to the Infanta at once and requested a free day in order to pay a visit. Doña Maria remembered the hints thrown out by the Count de Luna and immediately suspected that her lady-in-waiting intended to meet a young lover, and not an old abbess. The Infanta's first impulse was to refuse the request. But after further reflection she came to a different decision. If Doña Leonor was deceiving her, she wished to find this out. She therefore graciously granted the request, even offering one of her own coaches for the journey to the convent. But she gave secret orders to the coachman to watch Doña Leonor's every step and not to let her out of his eyes for a moment.

III

At the appointed hour Doña Leonor arrived in front of the convent and was conducted to the room of the Abbess. When she drew back her veil in order to kiss the old lady's hand, the Abbess could barely conceal her emotion. Doña Leonor's face showed traces of grief, yet she appeared strangely transfigured, as if she had already been touched by the wings of fate. Her eyes glowed in her pale face with an expression of suffering but also exaltation. Was this really the same girl whom she had released from her guardianship barely a year before?

The Abbess gently enquired about her well being. Doña Leonor assured her that she lacked nothing, only she felt a little lonely at court.

The Abbess was silent for a moment and then expressed her surprise that Doña Leonor had been accepted back into the court, as her first visit had not been too successful...? But again Doña Leonor, lowering her eyes, gave the evasive answer, that as far as she knew, a position had unexpectedly become available.

The Abbess, somewhat taken aback by the lack of candour shown by her pupil, which was something new to her, now decided to set an example by proceeding with openness on her part. 'To be sure', she replied, 'and I know also exactly why this position was offered to you. Fortunately there are those who have confided in me more than you have done.' Whereupon she drew forth the letter from Doña Clara and read out its contents.

Doña Leonor's eyes widened with horror as she listened. 'How could she...how could she bring herself to...' she gasped, in utter confusion. In vain did the Abbess seek to reassure her that not a soul would ever learn what Doña Leonor's mother had confided to her. The girl was not to be pacified.

'Why is she interfering?' she lamented. 'Why can she not leave me in peace?'

'She is concerned for your future, child', replied the Abbess solemnly.

Doña Leonor remained silent and pensive. When she eventually spoke, she admitted: 'In only one respect has my mother put me to shame. And this is by confiding in you. I should have forestalled her. If I have remained silent, it was only to spare you, to avoid troubling you. But now I can no longer remain silent. I will confess all to you as if on my deathbed, and you will understand that my fate is sealed.' She then seated herself at the feet of the Abbess and began to relate her story.

'You know that when I left you and the convent it had been my sole wish to return as soon as possible. I was afraid of the world outside – in my heart I revolted against it. Had my mother not pressed me so hard – and had you not advised me to put my resolve to the test by going out into the world and meeting people, before deciding to enter the life of the convent... You were right, Mother Superior, I know that now, but at first I found it so very hard to follow your wise advice. I did not know how to conduct myself in society – everywhere I went I felt lost and a stranger. And my mother was leading such a hectic social life at this time. She was particularly eager to invite gentlemen who were rich and unmarried. How many embarrassing scenes I had to endure, how many evenings of torment! But at least on our estate I could occasionally find a place of refuge where I could be alone. It was worse when my mother brought me to Zaragoza. The court appeared to me like a brothel. Everywhere I went I was conscious of the men's lustful glances. I am always being told that I am beautiful. But what a burden this beauty can be if it attracts nothing but vile behaviour and depravity. It was then, Mother Superior, that I became convinced that this world was intolerable to me and that I was destined for the convent.

But then came the day when I first set eyes upon him... It was at a singing tournament, and he was the winner... Oh, how impoverished is human language! I wish I could describe it in the language of an angel, how he sang, how his voice resonated in my heart... It was I who set the crown of laurels on his brow – how that happened, I will never know. Had anyone told me beforehand that I would have the audacity to stand up, before the entire city and risk offending the Infanta by acting in defiance of her wishes... and yet this is what happened, as if in a dream, as if I were being guided by a higher power. Oh, if only you had seen the look he gave me when I presented him with the wreath! It was then that my life truly began. Everything that had gone before seemed to have vanished into a mist. I knew nothing of this man and yet he seemed more familiar and closer to me than anyone I had ever met before. I told myself that I would never see him again, but in my heart I could not believe it. I kept seeing his face before me, I kept hearing his voice. For the first time I understood what you meant when you spoke to me of being tempted by life. During the following days I begged God to make me forget him. But gradually it became clear to me that actually I did not wish to forget him. Even were he to remain for ever a stranger to me, the very thought of him would be a sweet consolation, knowing that he existed, somewhere in the world! I returned home to the routine of everyday life. But within me there lived a hope that sustained me, allowing me to forget all the hardships I had previously endured, the social gatherings, the strange gentlemen, my mother's remonstrations…

And this hope was not in vain. One evening I found a letter in my chamber – by what means it got there I will never know. Yet I knew at once that it was from him. Oh, dearest friend, what joy! He wrote that after the singing tournament he could not forget me, that since then he could think of nothing else but me. However, he did not dare to present himself openly to my family because he was fighting on the side of the rebels. He was thus obliged to write to me in secret – and then he asked whether he might hope that his love might be returned, just a little. As if he could have any doubt! As if he had not seen in my eyes what I saw in his! And that is what I wrote to him, that very same evening. I told him all that I felt for him. I know, Mother Superior, that I should not have written thus to a strange man. I should have restrained myself, in the manner of wise and virtuous women. But I was far too happy to behave in a wise and virtuous manner. That evening I felt my existence to be bathed in a glowing light.

He had described to me a place where I could leave letters for him and where I would find his to me, in a hollow tree at the edge of the cemetery. There I brought my answer next day, and from there I collected his letters. They were wonderful letters, Mother Superior. Through them I began gradually to learn about what kind of person he was and what kind of life he led. He comes from a small mountain village, where he grew up alone with his mother. How vividly he described this mother, and how lovingly! It was she who taught him to sing. Apparently she had herself once earned her bread as a singer. He had worked the farm with her until, to please a friend, he had joined the army of the Count d'Urgell.

I can see from the look on your face what you are about to say: that he is of humble origins – that I would be betraying my class by becoming his wife. But in my eyes Manrique does not come from a lower rank. He seems to me like a prince in a fairy tale who has been cast away or exchanged in the cradle. And I am not the only one to think so. The Count d'Urgell holds him in high esteem; only recently he has promoted him again. Many believe he is destined for higher things. True, he is still poor, but so am I. And you of all people, Mother Superior, will surely agree that the true nobility of a person does not lie in owning property. If skill and honesty could earn a noble title, then Manrique would bear the noblest coat of arms!

For many weeks I had to be content with his letters alone, conveyed, it seems, by various couriers to that tree. But then he wrote that he was being sent by his commander on a mission to this neighbourhood, and that he wished to see me again. He suggested the grounds of our estate as a meeting place, as my honour would not be compromised there, for if he should approach me too closely I could always cry out for help. Unnecessary caution! I have never doubted his sense of chivalry – I would have followed him into the deepest of forests.

Since then there have been several nights when I crept out to him in the park, clothed in the soft gown that is his favourite because I wore it when first he saw me. Mostly he came for a brief hour, making a detour when his duty took him to neighbouring villages. But sometimes he was granted several free days – at Christmas it was a whole week. Oh Mother Superior, what a time it was! I only came alive during those hours with him. By day I was like a sleepwalker, I barely took in what was happening around me. It is little short of a miracle that no one guessed my secret long before. Once my mother came to the door when I was reading a letter from Manrique – I barely had time to hide it. Another time, as I was about to creep out of the house, I almost collided with one of the servants – I thought my heart would stop!

But it was not any of the servants who discovered us, nor was it my mother, but… You are aware of what happened at Easter, what I had long feared. My mother's efforts to find a rich bridegroom for me were at last crowned with success. This Count de Luna – I instantly had my suspicions when I saw the way he looked at me. He wants me to be his wife, and he is accustomed to getting what he wants. And it is this very man who knows about me and Manrique! He followed me – he saw us together – he intends to kill Manrique, Mother Superior! And he is so powerful, and has so much influence. To make me a lady-in-waiting at the court of the Infanta was child's play to him. And I live in great fear that this is not all he has in mind for me. God knows how unwilling I am to be at court, among these hard, malicious people, but I would gladly remain there if only nothing would happen to Manrique! I suffered before when I knew him to be fighting in the front line, or travelling in enemy territory where at any moment he might be recognised and taken prisoner. But what are the dangers of war compared with this terrible Count de Luna! Perhaps he is already plotting to have him murdered while we are sitting here, unsuspecting. Dearest friend, I can barely sleep at night! Only one thought sustains me: that Manrique's fate is mine also. Should he die, I also will die. And if God wills that he remain alive, then I also will be glad to live.'

IV

At this juncture Doña Leonor ended her story. It has been rendered here as a smooth flowing narrative for the sake of brevity, whereas in reality it was frequently interrupted, by questions, contradictions and even exclamations of horror from the Abbess. And in reality the narrative did not reach a conclusion, but rather developed into a lively debate between the two friends. The Abbess used all the arguments at her disposal to demonstrate to Doña Leonor the madness of her actions. She implored her not to throw herself away on a rebel and adventurer, merely because he had appeared in such a secret, romantic manner, was handsome and in possession of a fine voice. What did she know of this man? Only what he thought fit to tell her. He could offer no family background which could have shed light on his character, nobody to vouch for him, no respectable reputation. If Doña Leonor was determined to reject the Count de Luna's offer of marriage, no one could force her to marry him – God forbid! But may heaven protect her from entering into an alliance in haste, which might destroy her entire life! But Doña Leonor continued to insist that her fate was already sealed by a higher power and vowed passionately that she would remain true to Manrique unto death.

In the evening, when the two women parted, they were still far from reaching any agreement. But in the course of a sleepless night the Abbess finally resolved that come what may, she could not withhold her motherly support from the inexperienced young girl. For the very reason that Doña Leonor was so deeply affected by her emotions, it was all the more important to prevent her from being carried away by them entirely. Thus the Abbess wrote to her former pupil the following day, assuring her of her renewed friendship, but begging her at the very least to keep her informed of developments. And Doña Leonor, moved and grateful for her affection, promised the old lady that she would hand over to her at once any communication that she received from Manrique.

It was some weeks before any news came from him. Doña Leonor had told her beloved of the change in her situation, but in the Aljafería where there were a thousand spying eyes, it was difficult to exchange secret messages. However, Manrique eventually managed to smuggle a note to his betrothed – Alfonso, his best friend, pressed it into her hand in a crowded alleyway, having hung around for several days awaiting this opportunity. It contained little more than an assurance that he was well and loved her as much as ever, and telling her where she would find any further messages or could leave any; not this time in the hollow of a tree, but in a crack in the wall of an old solitary chapel. The Abbess, to whom Doña Leonor immediately gave the letter, was unable to form any opinion about his character from reading it. It displeased her that he had chosen a house of God as the place for the exchange of secret letters, but she could not help observing that she had never seen her young friend so happy.

Manrique subsequently sent several more messages to his beloved. Doña Leonor diligently, even proudly, carried them all to the Abbess and read them aloud to her, many times over, discovering in every phrase evidence of his noble spirit and heroic attitude to life. Little did the two women suspect that there were others beside themselves who were enjoying reading Manrique's letters. The Infanta was naturally disappointed with the coachman's account of Doña Leonor's first visit to the convent, as she had hoped to catch the girl indulging in underhand behaviour. However, since then she had found a way to take advantage of Doña Leonor's close relationship with the Abbess. Although the coachman was unable to hear what passed between the two women when they were inside the convent, he gleaned certain items of interest when they took leave of each other at the gate and conveyed these titbits to his mistress.

Soon he was able to inform her that Doña Leonor was in receipt of secret letters. Doña Maria had her chamber searched and they found, carefully sewn into a cushion, not only the short messages that Manrique had recently sent her in Zaragoza but also the much more detailed letters that he had sent via the hollow tree in T. This small bundle of yellowing papers was for Doña Leonor a precious momento from which she could not bear to be parted. Not only did these letters document the various stages of their love affair, but also, what was more crucial to the Infanta and Don Nuño, they contained certain details about the village Manrique came from, about Manrique's mother, and Manrique's journeys in the service of d'Urgell. The Infanta had every letter copied, word for word, and then the entire bundle was replaced, exactly as it had been found. And while Doña Leonor believed her secret to be safe, it was passed on to the Count de Luna, and was filling up a dossier, all the more rapidly, as Lieutenant Gomez had not remained idle, and had communicated to his employer every detail he could discover about Manrique Corda.

Soon the day came when all this effort was rewarded. In the late summer, after months of stalemate during which both sides in the civil war held each other in check, the two armies confronted each other near the small town of P. A battle was about to take place which would in all likelihood determine the outcome of the war.

The Count de Luna had meanwhile been promoted yet again and now commanded a regiment, which was stationed in the woods in front of P. From his tent he could see the city walls and on their battlements the standards of d'Urgell, who lived as a prince in the city. But what did the usurper's audacity matter compared to the question of whether Manrique Corda was also residing within those walls? Don Nuño knew that the Count d'Urgell trusted him above all others and that he gave him the most dangerous missions as a curier. Perhaps he would be sent on such a mission before the battle of P. again? Don Nuño had his men questioned as to who among them had been present at the singing tournament of Zaragoza and who had seen Manrique Corda. A handful of such men were found and they were placed in position in front of the gates of P. For a whole week nothing happened and the Count had almost lost hope, when one morning the news was sent to him that two muleteers, heavily laden with goods, had left the town travelling northwards and that one of them resembled the man in question.

Don Nuño reflected. The information was rather vague. Apparently the sentinel was not certain of the man's identity, as it was more than a year ago since the singing tournament. The men had left through the north gate? One glance at the map revealed to the Count that not far to the north the roads forked, and one of them led in the direction of the mountains where his rival's village lay. The Count had learned from the intercepted letters that Manrique used every opportunity to visit his mother. The sentinel's suspicion was not unfounded. The Count gave orders that the two men be secretly followed. If they did not take the road leading to the mountains they could be left unmolested. But if they did they would need to find quarters for the night, and then they would be sitting in a trap.

Everything happened just as the Count had forecast. The two muleteers did take the road leading towards the mountains, and at the onset of darkness they did take up quarters for the night in a farmhouse. The man who had been following them rode back in haste to P. to inform the Count, who was filled with glee: at last they had succeeded! They had caught him, the man he so hated, who had dared to raise himself above his station. He would not escape the Count's revenge, and if, as was likely, he turned out to be carrying secret messages on behalf of the Count d'Urgell, then this revenge would also be regarded as a triumph for the rightful king!

Don Nuño set off with a heavily armed troop of men and, led by the messenger, reached the simple farmhouse shortly after midnight. He imagined his rival lying asleep in his bed, unaware of the danger. But his hopes of an easy capture were to be dashed. As luck would have it, the farmer, to whom the place belonged, himself a secret follower of the Count d'Urgell, suffered from pains in his joints and could not get to sleep. Turning restlessly in his bed he suddenly thought he could see a light outside the window and a shadow flitting past.

In a flash he realised what this meant, and he hastened to the chamber where Manrique and his friend Alfonso Ruiz were asleep. Starting up in shock, the two threw themselves into their clothes. The farmer showed them to a side door leading directly to the stable, but Manrique, fearing that the house was surrounded, refused to flee before burning the documents with which his Commander had entrusted him, and which would have caused great damage had they fallen into the hands of the enemy.

Precious seconds passed as they searched for a tinderbox, and just as the letters went up in flames the front door was forcibly kicked in, and the Count's men pushed their way into the house. The farmer, clad in his nightgown, stumbled towards them, asking sleepily what they wanted. Attempting thus to detain the soldiers, he gave the friends time to slip out through the side door and into the stable.

Meanwhile inside the house Don Nuño had pushed the farmer aside, who was complaining loudly about his broken door. But despite the noise, the Count thought he could discern the sound of a door closing. Ahead of his men, he swiftly searched through the house, discovered the bedchamber that had been so hastily vacated and finally the side door. He stepped outside and looked all around. There was no one to be seen, nothing to be heard other than a soft neigh from the stable immediately opposite him. Were the traitors hiding in there?

Don Nuño beckoned to his men and tiptoed towards the door

of the stable, when just at that moment the door was violently pushed open and a man could be seen astride a carthorse, while a second man, who had opened the door, swung himself up into the saddle behind him. The Count was standing barely five paces away and could see the face of the rider quite clearly: it was the face that he had seen in the moonlit grounds of T., the hated face of Manrique Corda!

Without thinking, Don Nuño leapt forwards, drawing his sword from the sheath.

As Alfonso Ruiz was now in the saddle, Manrique was about to spur on the horse, when he fatefully cast a sideways glance at his attacker. Their eyes met and now it was Manrique who recognized the other man. In his astonishment at this unexpected encounter, he hesitated for an instant, and the Count, taking advantage of this hesitation, leapt upwards and plunged his sword into his rival's chest with all his force.

Bleeding heavily Manrique sank down in the saddle, but Alfonso Ruiz swiftly seized the reins, spurred on the horse, and galloped off into the darkness, bearing the body of his friend, while the Count shouted at his soldiers not to let the accursed traitors get away. But most of them were inside the house, only a few having been posted outside. Two of them did draw their swords in an attempt to bar the rider's way, but Ruiz, with a daring manouvre, managed to evade them and rode away, holding Manrique's lifeless body in the saddle. Their pursuers hastened to mount their own horses but soon realised that there was little hope of catching them, in view of the darkness and the difficult terrain.

Don Nuño cursed at this failure of his plan. The second bandit had got away, the letters that he was probably carrying on him were lost; even the farmer who had sheltered the two had slipped away in the confusion. But what galled Don Nuño most was that Manrique's corpse had also been spirited away. He would have liked to strike off his arrogant head and have it mounted on a stake, so that all of Zaragoza could see what had become of the feted victor of the singing tournament – so that Doña Leonor could watch as the vultures devoured the man whom she had preferred to the likes of a De Luna! And now this wretch would receive a decent burial, an honour he did not deserve!

But what did this matter as long as the man's heart had ceased to beat? His rival was dead, he was most certainly dead, and this consoling thought was the most important result. Now Doña Leonor must see sense and become his wife.

V

It was little less than one week later when the battle of P. took place, and the court of Zaragoza was rife with the most contradictory rumours; at first it was declared that the rebels had won, then that the troops of the king were the victors. But one thing was beyond doubt: it had been a most bloody battle and had cost innumerable lives on both sides.

Eventually the news came that the rebels had not only been beaten, they had been annihilated. True, the Count d'Urgell, together with the remnants of his army, had fled to the mountains and taken refuge in the fortified castle of Castellar, but as far as could be judged, he was no longer in any position to lay claim to the throne. It had been a great victory for the rightful king. The entire court indulged in an orgy of patriotic triumph and although Fernando wanted to delay his actual coronation until his adversaries had finally been vanquished, great celebrations were being prepared, with feasting, music and fireworks.

Doña Leonor was sick with anxiety. She waited day after day for a message from Manrique, hoping that it would allay her fears for his life, but she heard nothing. Her mother, on the other hand, soon received a detailed letter from the Count de Luna, in which he informed her of his imminent return to Zaragoza. With the greatest satisfaction he waxed at length on the triumph of their just cause, and expressed the hope that he would be equally triumphant in the battle to win the lady of his heart. He wrote that for his part he had removed the obstacle that stood in the way of his happiness – what could he have meant by that? – and, trusting that the gracious lady whom he addressed had also done her best to exercise her benign influence in guiding her daughter in the right direction, he was looking forward with confidence to the wedding.

Doña Clara found herself in a delicate position. True, she knew nothing of Manrique, but she was in possession of letters both from the Abbess and from her daughter relating to Don Nuño's suit, and in this respect she was quite clear in her mind as to the situation. The Abbess had answered Doña Clara's letter, regretfully informing her that there was little prospect in the near future of an alliance linking her family to that of the Count de Luna. As a suitor the Count might indeed have all the right qualities, but Doña Leonor did not love him – indeed, she seemed to have a strong aversion to him, unreasonable as it might seem. In such a case, the Abbess explained, any attempt to apply external influence, however well meaning, would be useless, furthermore, any attempt to coerce a girl of such sensibility could have devastating consequences. Doña Leonor expressed herself far more decisively and emphatically: she would rather die, she declared, than become the wife of the Count.

Doña Clara at once sent a note to Don Nuño, requesting him to visit her in T., before he travelled on to Zaragoza, so that they could consult together on the best way to proceed. Of course she did not wish to dampen the Count's confidence, just as she did not wish to dampen her own hopes of gaining such a son-in-law. But she thought it advisable to give him a hint that some time would elapse before a happy outcome could be obtained and that the present position called for caution and for a delicate approach.

Unfortunately the note failed to reach Don Nuño at his post. He had hastened on towards Zaragoza on a mission for the king. The result was just what Doña Clara had attempted to forestall with her letter: the Count arrived in Zaragoza, presented himself in the Aljafería and when he greeted the Infanta Maria she inquired gleefully whether he did not wish to see his betrothed.

After a brief hesitation Don Nuño assented. But as they were about to summon Doña Leonor, he prevented them, explaining that he would prefer to go himself and speak with her in private.

The Infanta, with an ironic smile, declared that she quite understood that the lovers wished to be alone together, and told the Count where he would find Doña Leonor. This was in a beautiful arcade in the inner courtyard of the Aljafería. A chorus of the court ladies was practising the songs that they would sing at the victory celebrations and among them Don Nuño recognized the lady he sought. Overcome by his feelings, he remained standing beneath an archway in the arcade. Doña Leonor looked to him even more beautiful than he had remembered. How noble was the pallor of her skin, how pure the look in her eyes and how soulful her expression! How she outshone the vulgar women surrounding her! Had the world anything more precious to offer than the possession of this divine creature?

But now she had noticed him also; although she grew yet more pale at the sight of him, she at once broke off the song in the middle of a verse, left the chorus of ladies and led the Count towards a secluded alcove where they could speak undisturbed. His heart beat violently as he followed her. The manner in which she had received him seemed encouraging. So he addressed her as if there had never been a Manrique Corda, paying her a gracious compliment. But Doña Leonor cut him short and asked quietly, her words faltering, about the battle of P. What had been the outcome? Who had been killed? And at the next moment, without even realising it, she spoke the name of Manrique Corda. Was Manrique Corda still alive?

The Count felt as if he had been brutally woken from a dream. He had believed his rival to have been vanquished. In the intoxication of victory he had ceased to think of him. But at this moment, with Doña Leonor standing before him, her eyes full of fear, wringing her hands so violently that her knuckles were white, the dead man seemed to have a ghostly presence there. Don Nuño hesitated in his reply. In his bitter disappointment he wanted to hurl the truth at her in the harshest words, but his reason told him that this would hardly be the best way of winning her affection.

Meanwhile Doña Leonor had realised what his hesitation signified. Words were not needed.

'He is dead', she whispered.

He nodded his head in assent.

'Is this certain?' she asked in a flat tone.

'Quite certain', he answered her unhesitatingly and his eyes expressed the certainty that filled his heart. 'I myself saw him fall.'

Doña Leonor retreated a step, her eyes glittering; she stretched out her arm and uttered a piercing scream that shook the walls shattering: 'It was you – you killed him!' And before he could reply, she fell in a swoon to the stone floor.

In consternation the Count called out to the ladies, who revived her with water and brought her to her chamber. The Infanta's personal physician examined her and declared her to be in a dangerous condition. It was not so much the girl's physical, but rather her emotional state that caused him concern. Doña Leonor lay on her bed as one dead and would neither eat nor sleep. In vain did the Count de Luna visit her bedside – she did not vouchsafe him a word. In vain did the Infanta herself deign to visit the sickroom – Doña Leonor gave no sign of being aware of this honour. Even her own mother, who was speedily summoned, did not succeed in eliciting more that a fleeting, absent smile from the girl.

When almost a week had passed without any change in the girl's condition, Doña Clara resorted to one last desperate remedy: she sent messengers to the Carmelite convent, begging the Abbess for her assistance. The old lady, as soon as she had heard what had happened, at once ordered her carriage to be made ready and set off for Zaragoza.

Her appearance in the Aljafería caused a considerable stir, for she rarely left the confines of the convent. Paying no heed to the palatial splendour of her surroundings, nor to the presence of the royal family, she asked to be shown straight to Doña Leonor's room. She then politely requested permission to speak to Doña Leonor in private.

Everyone respectfully withdrew, and no one was ever to learn what passed between the two women. But when the Abbess had left, Doña Leonor, after days of silence, suddenly opened her lips to speak and asked her mother for a bowl of soup. This was the first nourishment she had taken since she had received the fateful news, and Doña Clara fell upon her knees, and with tears of relief gave thanks to God.

Within two days the physician was able to declare his patient to be out of danger and on the way to recovery. But the joy experienced by her nearest and dearest did not last long. No sooner had Doña Leonor regained her strength than she used it expressly to forbid any visit from the Count de Luna. There was worse to come: as soon as she was able to walk she approached the Infanta and requested her permission to leave the court, as she intended to enter the convent of the Carmelites without delay.

As was to be expected, the Infanta dismissed this request as 'mere foolishness', and Doña Clara brought all her maternal authority to bear in an attempt to dissuade her daughter from this decision. However, another authority came to the support of the girl, namely that of the Abbess. Her commanding presence succeeded in ensuring that the girl's wishes were not simply ignored. A letter reached Doña Maria, pointing out in gentle and courteous words, but with total clarity, that no worldly power had the right to detain someone who had been called by God. And the Infanta, despite the Count de Luna's tempestuous demands for her to intervene, had no desire to provoke a conflict merely on account of one of her serving ladies, aware that the Abbess had the power of the Church behind her.

It was far harder for the de Sesé family to give up the girl and forego the alliance with the Count de Luna. Not that Doña Clara did not feel gratitude and respect for the Abbess, but her ambition weighed far more heavily than these feelings; and in fact, her son, Don Guillén, who had also recently come to Zaragoza, denied point-blank that the Abbess had any right to interfere in his family's affairs, describing her angrily as a 'scheming ensnarer of souls'. Doña Leonor, barely recovered to health, found herself caught up in a passionate family conflict. But she displayed more resolution that both her mother and her brother had expected, and the Abbess continued to do all she could to strengthen this resolution.

After only a few days Doña Clara had to give up any hope that her rebellious daughter might change her mind. All she could do was to implore her to wait for a short space of time, to allow a brief postponement in case she might have a change of heart. But Doña Leonor, motivated by a lurking sense of fear, was in haste to bring the matter to a conclusion. Although the Infanta had reluctantly granted the girl's request to leave her service, until the matter had been finally settled, she was still occupying her chamber in the Aljafería, and she found the constant proximity of the court to be ever more oppressive. Don Nuño sent her notes almost daily, at first in a reverential, even modest tone, but which became increasingly angry and threatening. She hardly dared to leave her chamber, knowing full well that not only was he going in and out of the de Sesé's family quarters, but that he had more than once entered the Aljafería. Nowhere did she feel safe from meeting him, nowhere other than within the walls of the convent.

A few more letters were exchanged, but they no longer addressed the question of whether Doña Leonor should enter the convent, but rather of when she would. Leaving aside her mother's motives, the Abbess considered it only proper that the girl be given time to reflect carefully about such a grave decision. Therefore the time when she would make her final vows was set for three years hence. But until that time Doña Leonor was to live in the convent as a novice, preparing herself for her future duties as a nun. The Abbess was firm in her insistence on this, and the girl also begged for her mother's permission, until Doña Clara could raise no further objections.

Then came the day when Doña Clara had to admit her defeat to the Count de Luna. She repeated to him all that she had told herself, day after day: that much could happen in three years, that they would surely think of something to alter the course of fate, that perhaps there would be a further postponement… But she perceived that in his bitter disappointment the Count would pay no heed to such words of consolation. He sat before her with a stony countenance, looking as if his thoughts were far away. Little did she surmise that in his innermost mind he heard a distant, mocking voice: You will be rich, but you will never possess that which you most desire…

At last he got to his feet and threw on his cloak.

'Very well', said he 'if that is what she wants, she will get what she deserves.'

Doña Clara bowed her head. So this was the end of her dreams. Never would she be able to speak of her daughter as the Countess de Luna. The Count was renouncing his bride and no one could blame him for that.

But all at once Don Nuño banged on the table with his fist, rattling all the dishes. 'No woman shall reject a de Luna' he growled out between his teeth.

Doña Clara stared at him in amazement. His features were distorted and there was an angry glow in his eyes. She could not tell what his expression meant, what his words signified. But one thing became crystal clear to her: this man had no intention of giving up his bride. She opened her mouth to put an anxious question to him, but the Count had already turned from her and hastened away, his cloak billowing out behind him.

VI

In the Aljafería great preparations were under way for the victory celebrations. Everywhere there was the sound of running footsteps and people laughing, but Doña Leonor was barely aware of all this noise around her. She attempted to assuage the grief for her beloved with fervent prayers and by preparing her spirit for a life of abstinence and renunciation. Her curtains remained drawn, day and night, and hardly a sound was heard coming from her chamber. Her food was brought to her by a manservant and apart from her mother, he was the only person she saw. No outings or visitors were allowed to distract her during these final days of her worldly life.

Little did she suspect that there was a man in her close vicinity who bore news that could have changed her destiny. This was none other than Alfonso Ruiz, Manrique's friend. Doña Leonor had met him a few times when he had brought her letters from Manrique. She would certainly have admitted him, even though she would admit no other. But how was he to gain access to her, as he dared not have himself announced to her? He spent hours in the vicinity of the Aljafería. He paced along the streets through which Doña Leonor must pass if she left the palace. When this proved fruitless he attempted to slip past the guards in the train of a master tailor, which nearly cost him his life. He found out where her mother and brother were staying, in order to keep watch over their movements. But all his efforts proved in vain – he did not succeed in speaking to Doña Leonor. And thus, fatefully, he was unable to covey to her the news which he had come to Zaragoza to give her: namely that Manrique Corda, although severely wounded, was still alive.

Like the Count, Alfonso Ruiz had believed his poor friend to be dead, when he had fled with him into the mountains on the old carthorse. Manrique's body hung over the saddle, his wound bleeding so profusely that it seemed as if his lifeblood were draining away. With the Count's men in hot pursuit, Alfonso could do nothing for him. Only when dawn broke did he feel safe enough to halt. In a hidden clearing in the forest he tied the horse to a tree and laid Manrique gently on the ground. In quiet despair he gazed at the waxen face and the gaping wound – there could be no doubt, his beloved friend was dead. No amount of loving care could bring him back to life.

Alfons Ruiz was a sturdy son of a hill farmer and normally not easily moved to tears, but now they streamed down his face. From his early childhood he had looked up to Manrique with something like adoration, and in d'Urgell's army they had been inseparable comrades.

Finally Ruiz wiped away his tears and considered what was to be done. It was out of the question to leave Manrique's body unburied, at the mercy of wild animals, or, worse still, his triumphant enemies. It was only a short, though difficult, journey to the village where they had grown up together and Ruiz resolved to take his friend's body there, so that his mother could take her leave of him with dignity and lay him to rest in the earth.

He had already heaved the body onto his shoulder and was about to swing it crossways over the horse's saddle when a faint groan reached his ear. In horror he let the body slide to the ground. Was it a spirit breathing through the leaves? Or could it be that – Manrique was still alive? Ruiz bent over him in suspense and listened intently. There it was again, the faint groan, and it was without doubt coming from Manrique's mouth! He was alive, perhaps he could be saved!

Alfonso Ruiz tore his shirt into strips to get a makeshift bandage for the gaping wound. Then he lifted his friend carefully onto the horse, swung himself into the saddle and rode on, as swiftly as circumstances allowed. The path was uneven and frequently led steeply up the mountain side. The horse, unused to being ridden, was now exhausted and soon refused to carry the double burden. Alfonso had to dismount and lead it by the reins. The last stretch of the way led over a narrow mountain pass, where to put a foot wrong would mean certain death. Manrique had regained consciousness, was groaning and beginning to move. Alfonso tied him fast with his belt to prevent him falling from the saddle, but every sound Manrique made gave Ruiz new hope and strengthened his resolve.

It was already far into the night when he finally reached their village with his burden. He softly knocked on the windowpane of a small, but well kept cottage. Someone struck a light within and in the window frame there appeared a face the like of which was seldom to be seen. It was the face of a middle-aged woman, faded and showing the signs of hard work. But there was a dignity and firmness in her features revealing a lively mind that had been broadened by education and travel. Only the eyes, together with the deep furrows around the mouth, testified that this woman had tasted more than her fair share of the sorrows of life.

This was Manrique's mother, Azucena by name, a woman who was not easily distressed; but when she set eyes upon her son in the pale moonlight, slumped in the horse's saddle, she was unable to hold back a cry. She sent at once for a woman skilled in herbal medicine who lived in the neighbouring village. And the very same night this woman succeeded in bringing Manrique back to life. He had indeed lost a great deal of blood, and had also suffered from the hardships of the journey. However, by a miracle the Count's sword thrust, although penetrating deep into his flesh, had not damaged any of his vital organs. After a few days he had regained consciousness and was on the way to recovery – due in no small measure to the self-sacrificing care of his mother, who would not stir from his bedside.

Manrique's first concern, once he was able to think clearly, was for Doña Leonor and the fear she must be suffering on his account. It so happened that Alfonso Ruiz was about to set off once more. In the meantime he had heard of the defeat at P. and wanted to ride as swiftly as possible to the fortress of Castellar and join the remainder of d'Urgell's garrison there. Manrique intended to do likewise, but he feared that it would be weeks until he had even regained half his strength. So he asked Ruiz to make a detour by way of Zaragoza and to inform Doña Leonor that he had been wounded, but was still alive. His conscience did smite him at making this request of his friend: not only was the detour arduous, but, after the defeat at P. and the Count de Luna's attack, it involved considerable danger. But Ruiz, who had only during the recent days become fully aware again of how dear to him Manrique was, declared at once that he was ready to undertake the hazardous venture.

Mention has already been made of his stay in Zaragoza and his vain attempts to meet Doña Leonor. But as he was about to give up and make his way to Castellar he had a chance encounter which caused him to change his plans once more. A man spoke to him in the street and invited him to partake of a glass of wine in the nearest tavern. It emerged that he had observed Ruiz wandering the streets of Zaragoza, luckily not suspecting his motives. He simply thought Ruiz was a vagabond, or a casual labourer, who for the sake of a gold piece would be willing to undertake any task, however outrageous. And as Ruiz was content to leave him under this illusion, the man, after a second glass, moved closer to him and asked softly whether he would be interested in earning a few extra ducats...?

Ruiz enquired what he would have to do.

'Ah, a trivial matter', replied the other, 'but a good deed for all that.'

All he had to do, the man told him, was to help prevent a young girl from entering a convent. The foolish creature was set on becoming a nun, but a high-ranking nobleman, who did not wish to be named, had other plans for her. His intention was to carry her off and bring her to his estate, where he would be sure to instruct her thoroughly in her true vocation. Of course the gentleman could not afford to be seen during the girl's abduction, nor could he use his own servants, as they would betray his identity. So he was seeking capable men who could keep their mouths shut, to help him to carry out the deed, and he was offering them the prospect of a princely reward.

Alfonso Ruiz had difficulty in controlling his reaction. Could it be that the girl in question was Doña Leonor? He had indeed heard rumours that she wanted to take the veil, but had imagined it as a remote possibility, and anyway he had believed that his news would have dissuaded her from following this plan. Cautiously he sought to learn more about the lady in question. She must be from a good family – possibly close to the royal family? And this mysterious employer must surely be a man of great influence if he dared to commit such a deed without fear of reprisal?

Lieutenant Gomez – for it was none other than he, the Count de Luna's henchman, who had spoken to Ruiz – laid a finger to his lips; he was not to mention this to any one! But one glass of red wine led to another, and before the grey light of dawn, Ruiz had discovered everything there was to be discovered, and furthermore had allowed himself to be hired for the task of abducting Doña Leonor. Having arranged a meeting point with the Lieutenant, he then left Zaragoza with all speed, riding in the direction of his village. This time he had a powerful horse and was well provisioned, so that he hoped to reach his destination by the following evening. It was indeed high time; for in only four days, on Sunday, when Zaragoza would be celebrating the king's victory, Doña Leonor would be entering the convent of the Carmelites and Lieutenant Gomez would be taking advantage of this opportunity to abduct her.

Meanwhile Manrique, far away and ignorant of all that had happened in Zaragoza, was sufficiently recovered to rise from his sick bed. Accompanied by his mother he was able to leave the hut and go for at first short, and then increasingly long walks. Here he knew every path, every stone. He had spent most of his life here amongst these meadows, and it was here that he had been happy – happier, as he now realised, than in the outside world. The mountain farmers, amongst whom he had grown up, earned their bread in a daily struggle with the forces of nature. They greeted him and his mother with warmth, even respect – a respect that had its own special reasons. Azucena had not been born in the village. One night, more than twenty years ago, she had suddenly appeared, a young woman holding a small child by the hand. She had taken up residence with an old gypsy, an eccentric, called Pedrillo. The two of them seemed to have known each other previously, although no one had discovered the true nature of this relationship, or what had moved the woman to renew it. In the course of time she had occasionally revealed a few things about her past to the neighbours: that she had been a travelling singer who through various misfortunes had lost her entire family, apart from her son, who lived with her, and that she had now settled down in order to bring him up properly, away from the dangers of life on the road.

The peasants felt that this story was somewhat incomplete, and possibly untrue, but they were far from condemning her for this. There were not a few among them who also had something to hide. At that time all kinds of smuggling took place in the area, and there were many skirmishes which had ended in bloodshed. These people were accustomed to a somewhat loose relationship with the law. They had understanding for a woman who wished to hide away from the world, and they posed no further questions as to her motives.

Furthermore, Azucena proved to be a hard working farmer. Old Pedrillo's neglected farm flourished under her care, and when he died a few years later, she carried on living there. From morning to dusk she laboured in the fields and garden, tended the animals, and kept the house clean. She also found the time to dedicate herself to the upbringing of her growing son. When she had declared that she wanted to bring him up properly, it was no empty boast, and the manner in which she did this astonished the neighbours. Not only did she teach him to read and write like a high-born gentleman, but she taught him to play the lute and to sing – romances, ballads, some well known, but some songs which were strange to their ears, such as had never before been heard in that part of the country. She herself excelled as a singer and in Manrique she found a gifted pupil.

Was there indeed anything in which this boy did not excel? His quick mind grasped all that she could teach him. He was able to put his hand to any kind of work. In riding or in fisticuffs he could hold his own with the strongest of the village lads, and when he occasionally sang his strange songs at the harvest supper or at a village wedding, they all listened to him, spellbound. The village girls adored this fine singer, who was also well built and a pleasure to behold. The lads were torn between admiration and envy. But there were those amongst their elders who secretly shook their heads and wondered what it was that made the boy so different. Where did his manner and all these skills come from? What was it that distinguished Manrique from the other lads? To be sure, his mother had come from afar, she was educated, had travelled extensively and had been able to impart knowledge to her son that was inaccessible to the others, but that alone did not explain the nature of his character. Azucena was a clever woman, but she was of a rather coarse build, indicating her gypsy origins. If one regarded her features and then those of Manrique, one could not help asking oneself how this mother came to have such a son and who the father could have been. Sometimes it seemed to the peasants as though they had an enchanted prince growing up amongst them.

Inevitably, Manrique, as he grew up, became increasingly aware of his gifts and his superiority. In consequence he could not refrain from displaying a little arrogance. Although he loved his mother dearly, he did not attempt to hide the fact that he had no intention of spending his life labouring on their miserable farm. For this reason he also showed no desire to marry a local girl, as his mother would have liked. From early on he expressed the wish to break free of the narrow confines of the village and to go out into the world. It was as if a powerful instinct told him that this was not his rightful place and that he must go away in order to find what was right for him.

Thus it was that he seized the first chance he could to get away. His best friend, Alfonso Ruiz, like so many in the area, was involved in smuggling, as well as being a mountain guide. One day he returned from one of these expeditions with the exciting news that war had broken out over the succession to the throne and that a Count d'Urgell was leading the rebellion. Ruiz was already determined to join the ranks of this d'Urgell, for not only did he pay good wages but it was also said of him that he stood for the rights of the poor, and offered any man, whatever his origin, the opportunity to gain fame and fortune. Manrique was carried along by his friend's enthusiasm and only too easily persuaded to become a soldier in d'Urgell's army – to his mother's horror, and to the disappointment of many a village maiden, but to the joy of Alfonso Ruiz, who swore to be a true comrade to him.

This had all happened less than two years before. Now he was back again, the village hero who had left with such high hopes. Had the Count d'Urgell succeeded in gaining the throne, he might have made Manrique a minister or a general. But the rebel army had been defeated and Manrique was lucky to have escaped with his life. What was there for him to do now – what was to become of him? Azucena was filled with such anxiety that she could hardly sleep at night. When she tried tentatively to discuss the future with her son he evaded her uneasy questions; but she knew him well enough to know that he would consider himself bound to the Count d'Urgell for good or ill and that he would not abandon him in his need. In the case of total defeat he would have no other choice but to try his luck over the frontier.

As things stood, they looked bad enough; but there was something else that struck fear into Azucena's heart: when she was about to wash Manrique's blood-soaked clothes, she found some letters in his inner pouch, letters written in a lady's delicate hand. Manrique had not confided to his mother that there was a woman in his life; hence she was not a little shocked when she held the proof of this in her hands. What sort of girl could this be who had won the heart of her Manrique? Was she worthy, was she capable of sharing his life – a life which in all probability would consist of nothing but danger and privation? Azucena could not resist the urgings of her mother's heart. In the middle of the night, as her son lay in the deep slumber of one recovering from a bad illness she drew the letters from his pouch and in the glow cast by the firelight read Doña Leonor's letters to her son.

When she had finished reading them and had replaced them in his pocket, her hands were trembling so violently that she could hardly retie the ribbon around them. The reason for her agitation lay not in the person of Doña Leonor – although she would certainly have preferred a sturdy peasant girl as a daughter-in-law to this delicate plant of noble offspring, who would hardly be suited to the hardships of life – but rather in a certain name that had struck her like a thunderbolt as she read it. She sat by the fireside, deep in thought, and as she gazed into the flames, various faces appeared before her, decades old, faded, almost forgotten; but now they had returned, filling her heart with fresh terrors, penetrating deep into her innermost soul…

Minutes, or hours later, Manrique woke with a start from his slumber – was it a ghostly breath that touched him, or was it a heavy sigh, like a groan? He raised himself up and saw Azucena still sitting by the fireside, motionless, as one hypnotised, an expression of horror on her face, as she stared into the flames. From time to time her chest heaved when she took a deep breath, as if she were suffering some great inner sorrow.

Her son looked at her with dismay. It was not the first time that he had seen her like that. How well he remembered certain nights during his childhood when he had been woken, as now, by a groan, a cry, a name whispered in horror, to find her sitting by the fire, as she was now, mesmerised by the flames, under the spell of a nightmare from which she could not free herself. What was she seeing in those flames? What kind of memories were they that would not leave her in peace? As a small boy he had asked himself these same questions, he had even attempted to put them to her, but she had always fended off his childlike requests, with a look of fear. He was too young, she had said, and her story too cruel to tell him. When he was a grown man he would learn it soon enough.

But as the years went by the peaceful, happy present seemed to triumph over the ghosts of the past. The strange fits that occasionally came over Azucena became less frequent until they ceased altogether. Why had they now returned? Had the danger he was in stirred some memory in his mother's mind? Would she now at last confide in him?

Such hopes gave Manrique the courage to disturb her reverie. 'Mother', he gently addressed her, 'dear Mother, may I ask…?

Azucena started up and turned to him. 'Manrique!' she exclaimed, slowly coming to her senses. 'Why are you not asleep, my son? You need your sleep now.'

'How could I sleep' replied Manrique, 'when my mother is suffering.'

Azucena gave a slight shake of her head, but her troubled expression gave the lie to her denial.

'And if she', he continued more forcefully, 'won't share her suffering with me.'

In torment Azucena turned her face away. 'Ah, Manrique!' was all her response.

Manrique got up from his bed, went over to her and very gently took her hand.

'Mother', spoke he, gazing intently into her face, 'why will you not ease the burden of your heart? Will you not reveal your secret to me at last? I am your son – and have I not always been a good son to you? Who, if not I, could stand by you in your battle against these terrible demons who have tortured you all these years?'

Azucena cautiously looked up. Her first impulse as she encountered the open, loving look on her son's face was one of withdrawal – that same defensive withdrawal that had hitherto sealed her lips. He was so young, so unsuspecting, so unprepared for the truth he would learn – no, no, she could not tell him. But then she thought of Doña Leonor's letters, of the name that she had read in them, and her conscience told her that she could no longer keep silent. Manrique had the right to learn the truth, however much it would shock him.

'Do you know the Count de Luna?' she asked.

Manrique gave an astonished frown. How had she come upon that name? That she might have read his letters did not occur to him at that moment – his thoughts were directed further back into the past. He recalled having once heard the name de Luna even before Doña Leonor had first spoken it. And suddenly it came to him: it was one of those mysterious names that had escaped Azucena's lips when she had sat by the fireside, barely conscious, wrestling with her demons.

'I do indeed know the Count', he replied, after a moment's hesitation. 'He is a man who does not wish me well.'

Azucena nodded slowly. 'That may well be so', she responded. 'His father also did not wish us well. Come, my son, lie down in your bed once more. The night is cold and you are still so weak. Lie down and I will tell you a story, just as I did when you were small. Do you remember? You always wanted to hear stories of ghosts and robbers. Now you shall have one that is about ghosts as well as robbers. Listen carefully...' She drew her chair close to his bedside and began to tell her story, softly but with deep agitation in her voice.

VIII

'Once upon a time there were two gypsies, mother and daughter, who roamed through the land with a group of travelling players. The daughter was a singer, and the mother had the gift of the second sight. They were poor but they earned their daily bread honestly, and their art brought wonderment and pleasure into the everyday lives of simple people. The daughter found a good husband, but she lost him to yellow fever after barely a year. All that remained of the marriage was her small son, who was cared for by the two women.

But one evening as all three were sitting peaceably by the fire, rough voices were heard in the camp. They were asking for the old woman, and before she had realized what was happening she was violently seized and led away by armed soldiers. In despair, the daughter, with the child in her arms, ran alongside them trying to find out what in all the world the old woman could have done wrong? But none of them would answer her.

It was only on the following day that she learned of the accusation laid against the old woman: she was accused of using witchcraft and having cast an evil spell upon a small boy; and when the daughter, rigid with horror, asked who had made this accusation, she was told: the Count de Luna. It was his men who had laid violent hands upon the helpless old woman; and it was his son whom she was supposed to have bewitched. The truth was that she had foreseen a dark future for him, just as she had seen it before her very eyes, but those people had been unable to understand this. In vain the old woman protested her innocence, even on the rack, in vain did the daughter throw herself at the feet of the Count. The court showed no mercy to the poor old gypsy woman. One terrible morning in the market place they lit the fire that was to put an end to her life; and her last cry before she was suffocated by the flames was to her daughter: avenge me!... avenge me...'

Azucena paused as she told her story. She was breathing heavily and her eyes reflected all the horrors of the scene that she could not put into words: the stake, the gaping onlookers, the shrieks of the tormented victim...

Manrique too was deeply moved. Now, finally, he believed he understood what memories must have been awoken in her mind at the sight of a blazing fire.

'And what did the daughter do then?' he asked in suspense.

'The daughter... she heard her mother's cry; she could still hear it long after it had died away. She heard it night and day, asleep she heard it in her deepest dreams: avenge me, avenge me... She could think of nothing else but this. Instead of returning to her fellow players she remained in the neighbourhood, together with her child, for days, for weeks, constantly racking her brain as to how she might carry out her mother's dying wish. She lived like an animal in caves in the woods, filling her child's mouth with berries, spending hours lurking in the grounds around the Count's Castillo, in constant fear lest the child in her arms should cry out and thus betray her presence. It was easy enough to gain access to the grounds: there was a gap in the back wall, large enough for an agile person to slip through. Nor did she have any trouble gaining entry to the Castillo itself. But there was a nurse-maid who was always with the Count's sons, even sleeping in their bedchamber.

But one day, shortly before the harvest festival, the gypsy woman observed the nursemaid leaving the Castillo, having no doubt been given leave to attend the festivities. Such an opportunity might not come again so soon. In the depths of night she managed to enter the innermost chambers of the enemy and seized the Count's younger son, an infant of about two years old. He was fast asleep in his cot and thankfully did not wake as she carried him in her arms, and disappeared with him into the woods, before anyone noticed that he had been taken.'

Manrique looked up at his mother in amazement. 'The younger son?' he asked. 'Not the one who had been the cause of the tragedy?'

Azucena looked away. 'No', she said, and an expression of unease flitted across her face, 'it would not have been so easy to carry him out of the Castillo. He was already six or seven years of age and quite a strong boy. He would certainly have woken up, it was just not possible... Everything had been thought through, down to the smallest detail...'

'But – what could the younger son...'

'And there was another reason', Azucena continued, not even hearing his question, and there was a wild glint in her eyes, 'to choose the youngest child of the family as a means of revenge: it was him the parents loved best – any casual observer could see that. If they lost him they lost the apple of their eye, their sunshine! Then they would experience for themselves the pain they had so callously inflicted on others. Oh, yes, that would be the perfect revenge...'

'The murder of an innocent child?' interjected Manrique, filled with horror, raising himself up in his bed. But at the very same moment it became clear to him that Azucena was not longer in a state to hear the voice of justice, of compassion, of reason – as far from it as she had been on the fateful day of which she was speaking. She was staring into the flames again, and her thoughts were totally entangled in the images of the past.

'Oh, that child!' she spoke in a feverish whisper. 'It was heart-rending, how he wept – how he wrung his little hands – called upon his father for help... Only the fire was already burning... the stake for the old woman... the dreadful smell of burnt flesh... Avenge me... just a single cry, hardly audible among all the voices... And then it was too late, the child was in the fire, burnt, burnt, my own child... The Count's son would not stop weeping... How could that have happened, my own child...? Burnt all over his body... beyond saving...'

She was now talking as if demented, her words rambling and disjointed. For some time Manrique had no longer been able to follow all that she was saying, but now the little that he had understood suddenly struck him with horror, as a yawning abyss opened up before him, making his head reel.

'What?' he cried, springing to his feet. 'What are you saying? Your own child lay in the fire, burned to death? And the Count's son – the Count's son was alive? But – but then – am I not your son?'

This question brought Azucena abruptly back to her senses. She started up, as if woken from a dream, and stared at Manrique, thunderstruck.

'You not my son!' she cried with burning eyes. 'Manrique, why do you speak so? Have I not always been a good mother to you? Have I not done everything for you?'

'Yes, for sure', Manrique stammered, 'but if it was as you said...'

'Ah, how can I know what I said! Do not trouble yourself about it, my son – come, lie down again and try to sleep.'

Manrique shook his head violently and tried to persist with his questions. But his mother refused to discuss the subject any further.

'Lie down again', she urged him repeatedly, as she attempted to force him gently back onto his bed. 'Sometimes I say crazy things, you know that… Lie down and sleep, we'll speak more of it another time…'

Manrique hesitated a while and then did as he was bid. He could see full well that Azucena no longer had the emotional strength to continue with her painful revelations. For the time being he would have to content himself with the insights she had allowed him. But he was determined to take her at her word and return once more to the painful subject as soon as the opportunity arose. He would not rest until the brief ray of light that had fallen, like a flash of lightening, onto the past, now more searing than illuminating, had been transformed into the clarity of total knowledge – although his heart pounded when he thought of the possible consequences for his own life.

IX

Manrique had assumed that he had more than enough time in which to penetrate into Azucena's secret, with all necessary caution; but fate decreed otherwise. Hardly had he sat down to supper with his mother the following evening, than there was a violent knocking on the door of the cottage and Alfonso Ruiz entered, covered in dust and exhausted from his journey. His face showed that he had some urgent news to impart. In astonishment Manrique sprang up and besieged his friend with a thousand questions: why had he returned so soon? How did things stand in Zaragoza? Had he – spoken to a certain person, and did he have a letter from her?

Alfonso looked into his friend's emaciated face with deep concern. How would he take the shocking news? No matter, he could not spare him. He sought to prepare his friend briefly, but then told him what was to be told: that Doña Leonor, mistakenly believing her lover to be dead, had resolved to take the veil; that he, Ruiz, had not succeeded in communicating to her the truth of the matter; and that the Count de Luna planned to have her abducted on the way to the convent of the Carmelites, which she intended to enter on Sunday.

Manrique sat for a few seconds, as if turned to stone. Then he appeared to be seized by a feverish, urgent impatience, as if in the very next moment it could be too late. He turned to his mother, requesting her to give him provisions for a long journey, for he intended to ride to Zaragoza that very night.

Azucena asked in astonishment whether he had been overcome by madness. How could he think of riding in his condition? And to Zaragoza, of all places, into the capital of his enemies! They would murder him, sick and helpless as he was! But Ruiz assured her that he would take care of her son and not allow any harm to come to him; and Manrique, pacing to and fro in the small room, like a tiger in a cage, did not give the impression that any objections would hinder him.

Thus Azucena had to admit defeat and allow the two men to go, although she did prevail upon them to stay the night and leave in the morning, to which Manrique reluctantly agreed. Ruiz's horse needed to rest, as he did himself; but above all, it was important for Manrique, still convalescent, to gather his strength for the arduous journey with a good night's sleep. Meanwhile Azucena secured the most docile horse that could be found in the village and loaded it up with all manner of provisions. In the grey light of dawn they said their farewells and the two friends set off.

On the very first day of their journey it became clear that Azucena's fears had been justified. Manrique, driven on by his fear of being too late, overestimated his strength. Towards evening he suffered a serious collapse. He was feverish, and had to lie close by the campfire, wrapped by Ruiz in blankets. During the night he started up again and again, and tried to get to his feet. 'To lose that angel' he muttered, turning his head from side to side in anguish, 'to lose that angel... to that monster...!'

At last, long after midnight, he fell into a fitful slumber and on the following morning he claimed to have recovered somewhat. The companions speedily continued their journey and were already cherishing the hope that they would reach their destination that same evening. But as the sun sank lower in the sky Manrique was overcome once more by a feverish attack and rendered incapable of riding any further. They set up their camp in a cave and lit a fire. Manrique was rendered inconsolable by his infirmity, and cursed the unlucky star under which he had been born. Ruiz, however, declared his conviction that all was not yet lost. If they set off early enough the following morning, he believed that they would still arrive in time.

But Manrique was unable to sleep a wink and hardly had a pale light appeared on the horizon than he woke Alfonso and insisted that they make a swift departure. Although he still felt weary and feverish, the strength of his will, strained to the utmost by the proximity of their goal, succeeded in holding his bodily infirmity at bay. He had difficulty in holding himself in the saddle, but despite this he drove his horse on with such speed that Ruiz was barely able to keep up with him.

This last stretch of the journey seemed like an eternity to the two friends. They had in the meantime resolved not to ride first to Zaragoza, but to head straight for the piece of woodland close to the Carmelite convent where Lieutenant Gomez planned the attack. Ruiz believed that he knew a short cut, but he mistook the way, causing them to lose a precious hour. At last they found themselves on the right path and galloped on towards the convent. The sun already stood high in the sky – they must make haste, or they would come too late...

Doña Leonor had meanwhile long since tied up her little bundle of possessions and was now outwardly as well as inwardly prepared to take leave of her comfortable bedchamber in the Aljafería, replacing it for ever with a bare cell behind the walls of a convent. She also had been barely able to sleep that night; over and over again she had searched her soul, thinking of the day ahead – the day which would irrevocably separate the past from the future. It was without regret that she cast a final glance at the familiar chamber, before quietly closing the door for the last time.

There was no one left in the Aljafería to whom she could say farewell. All had already poured forth to take part in the victory celebrations. In front of the gate an open carriage awaited her. It belonged to the de Sesé family and in the carriage sat Doña Clara who had decided at the last minute to accompany Leonor to the convent. She did not wish the Abbess to gain the impression that their daughter had fallen out of favour with her family because she had decided to take the veil; and Leonor herself should not part from her mother in anger. Hope still remained that during her novitiate the family might possibly still be able to exert some influence on the girl to change her mind.

Their route led them through the centre of the town, where the festival was already in full swing. The coach was forced more than once to make a detour, when meat was being roasted in the middle of the street or a juggler performing his tricks. The houses were festooned with flags, the people were clad in their best finery, and various small groups were commencing to sing merry songs. Doña Leonor, who sat bolt upright beside her mother in the back of the carriage, gazed down impassively on the activities of the crowds, as if far away in her thoughts. Her simple black robe and her pale face, marked by sorrow and renunciation, contrasted strangely with the gaily coloured scene around her.

They left the city behind them and came to a broad track which led directly to the convent. Now there was stillness all around them, broken only at intervals by the call of a bird or the song of the crickets. When they were already approaching the convent, the track narrowed and led alongside a brook through a thickly wooded ravine. But how to describe the travellers' astonishment when rounding a bend they suddenly came upon two horsemen barring their way, who with raised arms commanded the coachman to halt.

The coachman, who was an elderly, deliberate man, had no choice but to obey this command. There could be little doubt about the riders' intentions, as their faces were hidden by hoods with only narrow slits for their eyes. When the first horseman approached them more closely the outline of a cudgel could be seen beneath his garment. The coachman broke off a branch from the nearest tree; but before he succeeded in using it as a weapon, four or five masked robbers had suddenly sprung out from behind the trees. The horses shied, the women screamed, and the coachman, after a brief struggle, was overpowered by the robbers and thrown to the ground, where one of them plunged a knife into his chest.

On the seat of the carriage the women clung together in terror. With trembling fingers Doña Clara, trying to maintain her composure, loosened a golden chain from around her neck and held it out to one of the robbers, whom she suspected to be their leader.

'Here! Take it!' she cried, in a tone that, though fearful, was not without dignity. 'Take all that we have with us, but spare our lives, for the love of Christ!'

The leader – none other than Lieutenant Gomez, of course – took the necklace, casting a contemptuous glance at it, and dropped it into his pocket.

'Very pretty, my good woman', he retorted, 'but we are after something far prettier.' And as he spoke he cast an impertinent glance at Doña Leonor, who, shuddering violently, pressed deeper into her mother's arms. The Lieutenant grabbed her roughly by the shoulders and attempted to drag her from the carriage, but Doña Clara clasped her firmly.

'You wretch! You dare to…!' she shouted, and, her strength doubled by fury, she actually succeeded in holding on to the girl. But then one of the other robbers sprang from behind, seized her by the hair, and with one swift movement, cut her throat with his knife, so that the unfortunate woman expired, her warm blood flowing over the young girl.

This was more than Doña Leonor could bear. She gave a piercing scream and sank in a swoon to the floor of the carriage.

The cruel deed horrified even Lieutenant Gomez, hardened though he was. 'Are you mad?' he yelled at the murderer, 'Is this how you obey commands?'

The Count de Luna had in fact specifically impressed upon them they should avoid the shedding of innocent blood, if at all possible. But he had also made it clear to them that they must capture Doña Leonor, at whatever cost, and the Lieutenant intended to remind his employer of these words.

Gently he took hold of the unconscious girl and lifted her onto his horse while his henchmen plundered the dead and removed anything of value from the coach. But just as the Lieutenant gave the order to set off, the bandits suddenly heard to their horror the sound of horses' hooves. Two riders appeared round a bend in the track, only a short distance away, galloping at full pelt towards them.

X

Manrique and Alfonso were riding so fast that they were barely able to rein in their horses in front of the group of robbers; only then were they able to take in the scene that lay before them: the two dead bodies, the masked robbers and the lifeless form of Doña Leonor hanging over the saddle of Lieutenant Gomez. For a few seconds they were struck dumb with shock. Then fury took over, and as one man, they drew their swords.

'Cowardly villains!' cried Manrique, beside himself with rage. 'You wage war against women and old men – now show us how you fight against soldiers!'

The robbers blanched and dropped their booty. Although they greatly outnumbered the two, they were taken unawares by the sudden turn of events and so were totally demoralised. They were in fact little more than a miserable little band of petty thieves, unused to fighting and ill equipped with weapons, as they had not been expecting to encounter any serious form of resistance. One promptly slipped away into the woods, others brandished knives and cudgels ineffectually, while Lieutenant Gomez, who was the only one of them to present any threat, was hampered by the burden of Doña Leonor, as she lay over the saddle in front of him, and he did not think it advisable to let her drop. So, after only a brief skirmish, two of the murderers had fallen, and the others scattered in all directions. Only Lieutenant Gomez was left, still seated on his horse, holding Doña Leonor in front of him like a shield, so that the two friends could not advance on him.

Finally Manrique made him an offer.

'If you let her go', he suggested, 'we will let you go scot-free'.

The Lieutenant saw no alternative but to accept the offer. He rode a few paces in the direction of Zaragoza with his beautiful burden; then he let her glide to the ground and galloped away.

The two friends rushed to Doña Leonor and raised her from the ground. At first they had thought her to be wounded, even dead, until they realized that it was only the blood of her poor mother that covered her face and dress. So they laid her down on the bank of a brook and fetched water to revive her and to wipe away the blood.

After a little while she opened her eyes, and her first, faint glance fell upon Manrique. She recognized him at once, but her expression showed not the slightest surprise.

'Manrique!' she breathed, with a blissful smile. 'Oh, I knew it! Death is sweet...'

The sight of him had clearly left her under the illusion that she was no longer of this world but had gone to heaven to be reunited with her lover. Only when she also glimpsed Ruiz did she begin to wonder – and then gradually her memory returned, bringing back all the horror and the pain. Although the two friends hastened to explain to her how they came to be there, it nevertheless took a considerable time before Doña Leonor was in a state to comprehend the extraordinary turn of events. The fact that Manrique was not dead, as she had believed, that in consequence her resolve for taking the veil was thus rendered meaningless and that on the other hand the Count de Luna had attempted to thwart this resolve by violent means, all this threw the poor creature into a state of emotional turmoil; and when her eyes lit once more upon the carriage, in which the bloodstained corpse of Doña Clara still lay, her senses threatened to desert her once more.

Meanwhile they gradually became aware of the pressing question as to how to proceed further. Alfonso suggested that they conceal the victims' bodies temporarily by the side of the track and travel on to the convent, where they would report what had happened and request assistance. For in truth Doña Leonor was in need of aid, but above all, Manrique, whose strength had held out while action had been so urgently required, once this was over, now felt overcome by bodily weakness. He did have some misgivings about the advisability of delivering himself, a supporter of the rebels, to the mercy of a convent, but Doña Leonor vouched for the magnanimity of the Abbess.

So the three of them climbed into the carriage and travelled along the track leading in the direction of the Convent, Alfonso Ruiz taking the reins and the two lovers seated in the back of the carriage, still weak and exhausted from the horrors they had endured, but now safe and reunited once more.

At the same moment, Lieutenant Gomez, riding hard, had reached Zaragoza and was asking for the Count de Luna. He found him in the great square where tournaments took place, eagerly participating in the public games that were being held by the court in celebration of the King's victory. While the abduction of Doña Leonor was being carried out somewhere far away, as he thought, he wished his presence here to be observed by as many people as possible. When Doña Leonor was safely within his castle, he had planned to tell her and the outside world that he had rescued her from the clutches of unknown robbers who had intended to sell her into the Oriental White slave trade. Once they were married, nobody would think of questioning the truth of the story. Don Guillén, his future brother in law, had already been initiated into the plan and Don Nuño intended to tell Doña Clara the truth at the very next opportunity, so certain was he of her forgiveness.

As far as Doña Leonor was concerned, the Count had to admit to himself that his actions, even were she to believe the tale about the unknown abductors, were hardly calculated to gain her affections. But his burning desire to possess this woman, at whatever cost, suppressed the discouraging conclusions of his reason. It just could not be that a love such as his should remain unrequited forever! In his society, under his influence, Doña Leonor must surely tire of resistance and bow to her fate, realising that it was not within her power to change it; and once they had reached this stage, then it would only be a matter of time before the flames of his passion would ignite hers also.

The Count was indulging in such hopeful fantasies when, through the throng of the elegant, rejoicing courtiers, there appeared the burly figure of Lieutenant Gomez, covered in dust from his hard ride. At the sight of him the Count began to tremble with shock. At once filled with foreboding that his plan had failed, his first impulse was to avoid any appearance of being connected with the Lieutenant. He waited for a few moments, and while the attention of the public was caught by a particularly exciting bout of single combat, he strolled casually past Gomez as if by chance, muttering beneath his breath a meeting place.

It was a remote tavern, small and dingy, that the Count had chosen as a place for them to meet, reckoning that none of his acquaintances would be likely to frequent it. Barely a quarter of an hour later he was sitting at one of the grimy tables facing his henchman, and heard from him what had occurred in the wooded ravine near the convent.

Of course, the Lieutenant did not mention the fact that he had hired, of all people, a friend of Manrique Corda's, to help with the abduction. He spoke rather vaguely of treachery and unforeseeable events which had foiled their plans. However, Don Nuño's consternation at the extent of the disaster was so great that he did not delve into its causes. What he now learned, exceeded his worst fears. The attack had failed! His beloved was lost! His rival had arisen from the dead! And in addition to all this, poor Doña Clara had been senselessly slaughtered, this simple, ambitious woman who had wished for nothing more than to see her daughter a Countess!

Don Nuño's conscience smote him deeply, and he bitterly rued the day when he had thought up the plan for this wretched abduction, only now fully realizing its madness. How was he ever again to face his friend, Don Guillén? And how was he to appear before his Maker with this black guilt weighing upon his soul? For a few seconds it seemed as if he felt the hot breath of Hell upon him; however, it was not merely heavenly justice he had to fear, but earthly retribution, no less. Admittedly, he had played no part in the murders, had not even known that Doña Clara would be accompanying her daughter. But who would believe him? If everything had gone according to plan, society would have forgiven Count de Luna for carrying off his bride. However, the way things now lay, he must reckon with severe consequences if his involvement with this wretched affair were ever to come to light.

What was he to do? His reason bade him withdraw to A. directly, the very next day, and to wait upon the outcome of events from a safe distance. But how could he leave Zaragoza as long as Doña Leonor was still there, as long as he had no knowledge of her future fate? Where was she now? In the arms of this…? The very thought was enough to make Don Nuño's blood boil. Compared to this, what did thoughts of discovery and retribution matter, what did even the eternal fires of hell matter! You will be rich, but you will never possess that which you most desire… No, he would not withdraw from the scene like a coward! On pain of his very life he would not allow this villain to wrest his bride from him!

In the meantime Don Nuño resolved that Lieutenant Gomez should leave Zaragoza that very day; and these were the first words he uttered as soon as he was able to speak after hearing the fateful news. The Lieutenant raised objections, but this was merely to drive up the price. In fact, he had himself already entertained the thought that for him to tarry further in the city after this disaster would be inadvisable. The same afternoon he was to be seen on the road leading in the direction of Barcelona, carrying on him a great deal of money which he had got out of the Count, after some wrangling, although the Count bitterly resented having to reward this rogue for his crime. It may afford the reader some satisfaction to learn that in the end the Lieutenant did not escape retribution: about two years later, impoverished and down on his luck, he was convicted in Barcelona of robbery and murder and publicly hanged.

XI

At about the same hour that Lieutenant Gomez left Zaragoza for the last time, a novice from the Carmelite convent arrived there, bringing with her the news of the bloody attack, news which spread like wildfire and caused a great sensation. The people of

Zaragoza, their emotions already excited by the celebrations, thronged forth to visit the convent, until the city guards were finally forced to cordon off the scene of the crime. In the evening, as darkness fell, the mortal remains of Doña Clara and her coachman were brought back to Zaragoza; hundreds of people carrying flaming torches lined the streets, accepting without complaint the cancellation of the firework display, which had been planned as a finale to the celebrations.

For many days to come this remained the main topic of conversation in the houses and inns of the city. Rumours circulated which were listened to all the more eagerly as the official version of the story left many questions unanswered. What was this? A band of robbers had attacked the de Sesé's carriage? This news was a puzzling thing in itself, as no such band had been seen in the neighbourhood for many years. But if one did exist, the next puzzling thing was that its evil deeds were limited to an attack on one single carriage and on one which was only travelling a short distance. It would be on the road to Barcelona where traders would be journeying laden with money and goods that the prospects of rich pickings would be infinitely greater.

Of course, seated in the carriage had been Doña Leonor de Sesé, an enticing prey in her own right. It was said that she had been saved by the intervention of two brave men, who just happened to be passing that way. But who were these brave men? Why had no one set eyes on them? And what was the relationship between Doña Leonor and her ostensible saviours? She was known to be in the convent recovering from her horrifying ordeal, but she had apparently not yet entered her novitiate. All most mysterious indeed!

And if these were not mysteries enough: a trader who regularly delivered groceries to the nuns let it be known that ever since the day in question there had been a strange man staying in the convent. According to the trader this man was wounded and was being cared for by the nuns. Who could that be? One of the mysterious saviours? Or one of the equally mysterious robbers? Or both, in the same person, that is, an admirer of Doña Leonor who could not bear the idea of losing her to the convent? Perhaps she was not averse to being rescued by him? Still waters run deep, as is well known. Many remembered full well her appearance at last year's singing tournament, and in particular the ardent look that she had exchanged with Manrique Corda.

It was but a short step from this memory to the suspicion that the wounded man in the convent was in fact the victor of that singing tournament, the rebel Manrique Corda. Most certainly, this is how it could have been: Doña Leonor had refused to obey her family's wish that she marry a rich count. Angered by this, the family had resolved to put her in a convent. And in order to prevent this, Manrique Corda, for whom she had rejected the count, had attacked the carriage and murdered the troublesome mother. How romantic – but also how wicked! Now, the only question that remained to be puzzled over was the part being played by the Abbess. Would she stand by the sinful couple?

A consequence of all this gossip was that half the city turned out when a few days later the funeral of Doña Clara took place in the cathedral of La Seo. The great edifice had barely enough space to accommodate the vast crowds that poured in. But the absence of one person amongst the mourners was noticed: that of the son of the murdered woman, Don Guillén. It was said that he had been greatly affected by the death of his mother. The whole of Zaragoza had seen, in the evening after the attack, how aghast, how devastated, he had been at the sight of the bloody corpse. There were even rumours that he was preparing to cut short his promising career as an officer of the Crown, and to retire to the de Sesé's now abandoned family estate – a young man of true feeling.

But what about the second bereaved person, his sister – would she also stay away from the ceremony? If even only half of the rumours about her were true, she would have every reason to do so. Yet, just as the service was about to begin, a carriage drew up in front of La Seo, from which stepped two ladies clad in black. Both were heavily veiled, but were nevertheless instantly recognized: one was Doña Leonor, the other, the Abbess herself. A whisper travelled through the assembled crowd which, half shuddering, half respectfully, drew back before the newcomers, leaving the way clear for them to approach the bier. The choristers raised their clear voices in the requiem and the priest, approaching the altar, began to read the mass for the dead. But far greater attention was paid by the congregation to the two veiled ladies at the bier than was given to his words. Not that they gave the curious much satisfaction. The crowd was not even vouchsafed one glimpse of Doña Leonor's much vaunted beauty, for she did not once lift her veil, not even when she approached the bier to take final leave of her mother's corpse; and yet the people avidly followed her every gesture, as if expecting a sensation.

And they were not entirely disappointed. When the funeral ceremony had ended and the two ladies were about to enter their carriage, the Count de Luna suddenly barred their way. People nudged each other: this was the rejected bridegroom! Until that point he had been present at the ceremony, sitting on a raised platform amongst the nobility, not drawing any attention to himself. But now he had the expression of a man who was no longer able to control his emotions. The onlookers observed him laying a hand on the carriage door, preventing Doña Leonor from entering it, and saying something to her in a furious tone. Furthermore, they saw how the veiled figure trembled from head to toe, as if the devil himself had laid hands upon her.

The Abbess at once stepped between them, opened the door of the carriage and bade the girl get in. But she herself turned to the Count, and addressed a few words to him, so softly that no one but he could hear what they were. Their effect was, however, immediate. The Count gave a start, recoiled and looked around him with a nervous and sheepish look. Calmly, the Abbess now climbed into the carriage, which then moved off. The Count, however, who had remained standing there, exposed to the inquisitive gaze of the throng, pulled his hat down over his eyes and hastened away, like someone taking flight.

A day later an anonymous letter was delivered to the Prefect of the city, accusing the Abbess of harbouring a subject by the name of Manrique Corda, a vassal of the usurper d'Urgell, of hiding him in her convent and probably also even allowing him to be received by one of her novices.

The Prefect was a sober, sensible man. He knew the Abbess and held her in high esteem. Normally he would have thrown out such a denunciation in distaste, not wishing to soil his fingers with it. But what gave him pause for thought was the fact that it seemed to coincide remarkably with the rumours that had been circulating in the city during recent days, and as it was his official duty to investigate the attack near the convent, he decided to look into the matter. He asked for an interview with the Abbess and laid the letter before her, with the courteous request that she comment on it.

The Abbess swiftly cast her eyes over the document, her face betraying no emotion, and explained, as she calmly handed it back to him, that she had indeed taken care of a wounded man in her convent, but that he was no longer staying there. The Prefect was at liberty to search the place so that he might satisfy himself.

That would not be necessary, he answered, her assurance was quite sufficient for him. He would merely like to know whether the wounded man, to whom she had given shelter, was in fact the said rebel by the name of Manrique Corda.

'If a sick man is in need of our aid' the Abbess replied with dignity, 'we have no right to ask his name or beliefs.'

The Prefect nodded his head in polite acknowledgement. But perhaps she had something more to say concerning that rebel…?

'Nothing that would be in accordance with my conscience before God Almighty', was the Abbess's response, as she looked him straight in the eye.

The Prefect bowed and took his leave of her. He was, as has been said, a sensible man and following this conversation he felt neither the urge nor the obligation to pursue the matter further. Anyhow, he would not have found out more than that a day earlier at the crack of dawn, three persons had left the convent on horseback, two gentlemen and a heavily veiled lady, and that they had departed in the direction of the mountains.

Part Three
Castellar

I

The Count d'Urgell had once numbered amongst the richest men in Aragon. But now nothing was left to him of his estates but the fortress of Castellar, the last bastion of defence against the enemies who were closing in on him. It was to this fortress that he had withdrawn following the debacle at P. It was here that his last troops were entrenched, in the hope of saving whatever could perhaps be saved. He had long since given up all hope of victory or of gaining the crown; the superior strength of the opposing army was only too evident. His only hope was, if he could hold Castellar for some length of time, to win from his defeat at least acceptable conditions, not only for himself, but above all for his men, whose fate depended on his. Many had already deserted him once his luck had run out, but he was deeply moved to find how many had remained loyally at his side in these dark days. They were perhaps still secretly hoping for a miracle, despite the apparent facts, but reason must have told them that they were now fighting for a lost cause; and yet they were here, prepared to follow him, come what may. The thought that they might have to pay for their loyalty with imprisonment and death, pained Don Jaime deeply, and he prayed to God that he might be allowed to save them from this fate.

It was with such mixed emotions – he was touched, and yet troubled by his conscience – that he greeted the arrival of Manrique Corda in the fortress together with his friend Ruiz and his betrothed. Don Jaime had taken a liking to the young man from the outset. He had a good eye for talent, wheresoever it might be found, and so it was at their very first conversation, casual though it had been, that he had recognised how gifted and how promising Manrique Corda was, in contrast to most young men of his background. It had given him pleasure to encourage these gifts by giving him challenging tasks, and often, in those days of high hopes, he had imagined to himself what a boon a man of his calibre could be in the service of his fatherland.

And now the fall of the house of d'Urgell would also drag Manrique Corda into the abyss. Whatever the guilt of the lord, the vassal would not be forgiven. Why had he returned to him, from the safety of his village, barely recovered from his serious wounds? For him the war could have been over, and although he had lost his glorious prospects, at least he could have lived out his life in peace. Why had he come to this place when there was no need, to this place where all that awaited him was death and destruction? And why, moreover, had he brought his betrothed, a delicate and sensitive young creature, who had truly nothing to gain in the company of such rough men?

Manrique, however, remained deaf to such pleading. He had pledged allegiance to his lord and he would remain true to the end. As far as Doña Leonor was concerned, he was only too aware that this was no fitting place for her to be. Only where else was she to turn? Her mother was dead, and since then her brother had not communicated with her in any way. From his behaviour she must conclude that he had been involved in the Count de Luna's accused plan to abduct her, but she was reluctant to question him on the matter.

Manrique suggested to her that she stay with his mother, while the Abbess urged her to take refuge in the safety of the convent.

But Doña Leonor rejected both these suggestions and implored Manrique not to leave her. After all that had taken place she could not have borne a further separation. She would rather live in the shadow of death, would perform the hardest of tasks, if she would only be allowed to stay with him. She was even prepared to incur the displeasure of the excellent Abbess, who was not a little offended when her offer was spurned. Although upon her departure she assured her former pupil that the convent would in any case always be open to her as a place of sanctuary, Doña Leonor knew full well that the old lady deeply disapproved of her decision to accompany Manrique to Castellar. While she had tended to Manrique she had come to hold him in high esteem and trusted in his sense of honour; but that the girl was entrusting herself to a man, not even yet her husband before God, just as he was about to join a battle, which was doomed from the outset, seemed to her to be an act of such folly that it bordered on the wicked.

When Doña Leonor left the convent it was clear to her that there was no going back, and when she entered the fortress of Castellar at Manrique's side she experienced a kind of sombre satisfaction. So it was to be – thus she had willed it. Here she was, separated and divorced from the world, in a gloomy castle, the final refuge of an army that was already defeated. All the ties to her former life had now been sundered. Manrique alone remained to her, father, brother and husband, all in one. What now befell him would also befall her.

Fortunately there was in Castellar another lady of rank: Doña Isabel, the Countess d'Urgell. She had been living there as the mistress of the castle even before her husband had arrived, and afterwards was quite adamant in her refusal to leave. When she heard that Manrique Corda was accompanied by his betrothed and had been apprised by her husband of the couple's touching story, she immediately expressed the wish to make the young lady's acquaintance.

Doña Leonor was presented to her and the Countess d'Urgell, most favourably impressed by her beauty, her graceful manner, but above all by her love for Manrique and the courage with which she had dared to enter this warlike scene, all for his sake, at once took her under her own protection and had a pleasant room made free for her, close to her own chambers.

Meanwhile d'Urgell's scouts were bringing tidings that the royal army was approaching. The men in Castellar made haste to strengthen the fortifications of the castle in preparation for a long siege. Provisions were brought in, quarters for the soldiers were made ready and gaps in the walls mended. Manrique, who acted as his commander's right hand, was kept fully occupied by this work, so that Doña Leonor barely glimpsed him during the day. Yet she knew that he was always near, and this gave her peace of mind. The Countess d'Urgell, who was doubtless pleased to have female company in this rough place that was in keeping with her social standing, devoted herself to her with a cordiality that soon turned into the warmth of true friendship. The two women played their part in caring for and feeding the soldiers, applied themselves to their needlework, and took their meals together, while the officers ate with their commander at a separate table.

Only at evening time did the company gather together. There was a solar in Castellar which, although simply furnished, contained some board games and a few books. There was even an old lute, which Manrique soon mastered; and when he was asked by his fellow officers, or even by Don Jaime himself, to play his strange songs, the expression on Doña Leonor's countenance was one of total bliss. The war was far away, the Count de Luna was far away, the troubles and pain of this world were far away, and all that she wished for now was to halt the passage of time and to allow this period of harmony and security to last for ever.

Doña Isabel observed her friend's happiness and was deeply moved by it, but at the same time she secretly feared lest passion should triumph over the young lovers' virtue. Thus she began to hatch a plan which would enable them to get married without delay. In one of the neighbouring villages there lived a priest who was known to the Countess and whom she considered to be trustworthy. She sent a letter to this man, requesting him to visit the fortress while it was still possible, as in addition to the fact that several of the soldiers in the garrison were in need of spiritual comfort, there was also a marriage ceremony to be performed.

Doña Leonor acceded to her friend's wish, although she saw little sense in celebrating a wedding under such circumstances. How improbable it was that she and Manrique would ever survive the siege of the castle! The Countess could also see clearly the danger that beset them all; but if it were the case, she thought to herself, that only Manrique were to meet his death, it would be better for Doña Leonor to have the status and respect due to a widow than to be exposed to the contempt of the world in a dubious state of maidenhood.

In vain were these plans! Even before the Countess's letter had reached its destination, what they had been expecting daily now happened: the royal army arrived and encircled Castellar – at first this ring was widely spaced and loosely formed, but then it was made visibly stronger and tighter. Day after day new regiments arrived, well disciplined men bristling with weapons, all in good heart and sure of a speedy victory. Doña Leonor shuddered as she watched from the castle battlements, at the energy with which they set up their tents and began digging trenches; and she was horrified when she learned who was in command of these men: none other than the Count de Luna.

Indeed, it was so: the Count, whose regiment had distinguished itself at the battle of P., had been given the overall command of the royal troops besieging Castellar. He had not suffered any repercussions as a result of the attack outside the Carmelite convent. The rumours being spread by the townspeople had not affected him personally, nor was there to be any investigation by the authorities; and once he had established this, he began to make discreet enquiries concerning Doña Leonor. He soon found out that she was neither in the convent nor at the de Sesé family estate. Without doubt she had left with Manrique Corda, but where to? He did not imagine her to be in Castellar, but then the thought came to him that Manrique might have hidden her in his mother's village – as he had indeed considered doing.

Thus Don Nuño, barely had he been promoted to be Commander of the royal army, gave orders that Manrique Corda's entire property be forfeited to the Crown and confiscated immediately in its name, declaring him to be the intimate, and possible successor of the usurper d'Urgell. A troop of soldiers was dispatched forthwith to Manrique's village with orders to carry out the confiscation on the spot, and to convey any persons found on his property directly to Castellar, whither Don Nuño was now bound, together with the regiments under his command.

But hardly had he reached the castle when he learned that the besieged company included two ladies of noble rank: one was the wife of d'Urgell, the other the betrothed, or most probably, the mistress of Manrique Corda. Don Nuño, when he heard this news had difficulty in controlling his expression. Never would he have believed that Doña Leonor would go to such lengths for the sake of this churl. She had followed him to Castellar! She was prepared to endure the horrors of a siege! She had exposed her reputation to malicious gossip, surrendering all the privileges of her station! With what passion must she be inspired! Don Nuño stared up wrathfully at the walls of Castellar, walls which encompassed within them both the being that he loved above all else – and the one he hated above all else. Oh, he would raze those walls to the ground, would demolish the castle in its entirety. And she, who refused to become his wife, would now belong to him as his lowest slave!

But there was one final dagger thrust to pierce his wounded heart. Only a few days later a priest was arrested by soldiers on patrol as he attempted to enter Castellar through a gap in the ranks of the besieging army. As there was the danger of espionage, he was led directly to the Commander. The priest assured them that he was no spy. His sole aim in visiting the castle was to carry out his priestly obligations. Any devout soul who called for him had a right to request his presence. So saying, he placed the Countess d'Urgell's letter in his hands as proof of his statement.

When Don Nuño read that the priest had been called upon to perform a marriage ceremony, he had to restrain himself from immediately ordering the attack on Castellar. With a curse he tore the letter into shreds. If this wretched priest had achieved his goal... No, he could not contemplate the thought. The thought of Doña Leonor being that ruffian's lover was sufficient torment. She should never become his wife!

The Count issued orders for the priest to be put to the severest torture. He came in person to the torture chamber, and witnessed with grim satisfaction as the bones of God's servant creaked when he was drawn on the rack, and the walls resounded with his screams. On the following day he ordered that the man be tried for conspiring with traitors. It goes without saying that he was found guilty and that the sentence of death was carried out at once.

II

In the meantime the men who had been sent by Don Nuño to the mountain village which was the home of Manrique Corda, had after a toilsome journey finally reached their destination; but they found no 'property' which they could confiscate in the name of the King, only a whitewashed hut and within it a peasant woman, the mother of the said Manrique Corda. The hut was burned to the ground and the peasant women taken prisoner. This was what the Count de Luna had ordered, and if the soldiers failed to understand why they were supposed to deprive this poor woman, who could hardly be guilty of anything, of her meagre possessions and to inflict upon her the whole arduous journey to Castellar, they nevertheless did what they had been directed to do.

On a cold, already wintry, evening Azucena and her guards reached the encampment of the King's army. The Commander's quarters were situated in a solidly built, requisitioned farmhouse. The Count de Luna was dining there with some of his officers when the leader of the soldiers, a young sergeant, came to report that the mission had been accomplished and that the prisoner had arrived. He asked for orders as to what to do with her. The woman was ill, he explained with a note of pity in his voice; she had been suffering both physically and mentally ever since she had been forced to witness her hut being burned down. It seemed as if the sight of the flames had for some reason caused her mind to become disturbed.

93

Don Nuño had given no further thought to his decree concerning Manrique's property, the true reason for which had long since become irrelevant; yet now he was seized by a desire to set eyes on his rival's mother. He conferred briefly with his officers and then ordered the woman to be brought in.

The sergeant led Azucena in and it was clear for all to see that she was indeed very ill. She had been dragged from her village clad in only a thin garment, and when, deep in the mountains, the weather had taken a turn for the worse, she had been left totally exposed to the frosts. She was shivering violently with fever, and a racking cough tore at her chest. When she was brought before the Count de Luna, the sergeant had to support her, and as he and his comrades had done, so too did the officers seated at the table ask themselves why it had been necessary to bring this poor peasant woman all the way to Castellar.

At a sign from Don Nuño a chair was brought for the sick woman and a glass of water. Azucena sat down and drank the water with greedy gulps. Then she seemed to be somewhat recovered, and in a clear voice she answered the first questions the Count put to her. But no sooner was there mention of her village than her teeth began to chatter and she began to rave about a great fire. To all appearances she meant the fire that had destroyed her hut. In a wild panic she called upon her son to save their possessions from the flames – but at the next moment she saw an old woman burning, and then it was suddenly a little child kicking in the fire.

'My own child!', Azucena screamed. 'Hold her up, Manrique, untie the rope! There, her skirt is already ablaze! Don't let them, Manrique! Avenge me! Avenge me! My own child! And yet, how wonderfully this child has grown up in my care...'

The sergeant, who was embarrassed by this scene, attempted to bring the woman back to her senses, while Don Nuño listened to her words with a curious intensity, as if he could discern in them a deeper meaning. And indeed these delirious ravings did remind him of something: something far away, long ago, something horrifying, yet he could not quite grasp it... Then his manservant suddenly stepped before him, an old man who had been in service with the de Luna family for decades. Hitherto he had been quietly and discreetly serving his master at table; but now his expression revealed signs of agitation and a superstitious horror. He bent down to the Count and whispered a few words in his ear, at which the Count started up in horror, staring at Azucena as if seeing a ghost.

'See, Manrique, everything is burnt...' the prisoner babbled. 'Everything that we built up over years of hard work... the chests, our supplies for the winter... we are beggars, Manrique...'

The Count sprang up and stood in front of her. 'Woman', he addressed her haughtily. 'Do you not recognize me?'

The haughty tone was not without effect. Azucena shrank back and looked at him as one who has been rudely awoken from a deep sleep.

'No', she replied, uncertainly, 'who are you then?'

'The Count de Luna', Don Nuño answered. 'Do you know that name, woman?'

'The Count de Luna...' Azucena repeated, whose mind seemed to be wandering once more. 'But – that was an old man...'

'Quite right, there was an old man. But he is long since dead. I am his son.'

'His son...' murmured Azucena, as she struggled to collect her thoughts, 'that's right, there was the other son...'

'The other son? What do you know about it?'

But the threatening, penetrating tone behind the question caused Azucena to hesitate. Her eyes began to focus more clearly and her brain began to pick a way through the fog of fever. 'I?' she asked. 'What should I know of that?'

But just this brief moment of clarity had convinced the Count that his suspicions were correct. 'I had a brother', he spoke slowly and in a threatening tone, 'who about twenty years ago was carried off by a gypsy woman and murdered. Have you ever heard anything about that?'

'No...no...' Azucena stammered, with convulsive gestures, as if warding off something.

'Do you know who murdered him?'

'No!'

'Was it you', cried the Count in a terrible voice, 'who took his innocent life?'

'No! No!' Azucena sprang to her feet, staring around her with a hunted look, like a wounded animal. 'I did not take his life... I would never...my own child...'

'Do not believe her, my Lord!' the old servant cried out, no longer able to restrain himself. 'It was her – I recognize her again, no doubt about it! This woman stood in front of the stake on which they burned her mother to death as a witch! She is the one who murdered your brother – I will swear to it before all the world!'

Azucena let out a scream and fell to the ground in convulsions. The officers seated at the table were speechless with amazement. Most of them had heard of the tragedy that had befallen the de Luna family, and it seemed to them almost incredible that after all these years the murderer of the Count's son should be delivered to his brother by such a quirk of fate.

Don Nuño himself had great difficulty restraining his feelings of triumph and excitement. How right his instinct had been, when he had given orders to bring the woman to Castellar – and he had been well aware of the disapproval that his action had provoked. But now this would cease: he had not been confronting the mother of his enemy but a woman guilty before the law, a convicted murderess. What a twist of fate! With what emotion Don Nuño now remembered his murdered brother, remembered his father who had grown prematurely old and died before his time because of this tragedy. But now the time was approaching when justice would prevail and vengeance taken for the suffering of the old man as well as for the blood of his brother, shed so dastardly. Both of them would now be able to lie at peace in their graves.

He gave orders that the prisoner be put under lock and key and strictly guarded. She was to receive medicine and all the care necessary for her recovery. On no account must she be allowed to succumb to the fever before expiating her crimes in a fitting punishment. Already the Count was firmly resolved: as soon as the woman was well enough to be transported, he intended that she be taken to Zaragoza and tried before a public court. The execution should, however, be carried out in A., in the very same market place where once the old witch had been burned to death. Castellar would assuredly have been conquered long since, and should the son of the murderess have been taken prisoner by the victors, then, bound with iron chains, he would be made to watch his mother burn, just as she had once watched hers burn. Yes, then indeed would the circle be closed and the darkest chapter in the history of his family brought finally to an end.

III

Although the besieging army had now completely encircled Castellar, there were certain channels of communication by which the besiegers could learn about what was happening within the fortress. Likewise the rebels also could learn about what was happening outside the walls. So by the following day the Count d'Urgell had heard that in the enemy camp the mother of his captain, Manrique Corda, was being held prisoner and that a terrible accusation of child murder was hanging over her.

Don Jaime asked himself in astonishment what he was to make of this news. That the mother of his officer had been brought to Castellar, seemed in itself to be odd – at that time it was not yet customary to involve the relatives of your opponents in the conduct of the war – and that she was being accused of murdering the brother of the Count de Luna seemed almost incredible in these circumstances.

The Commander sent at once for Manrique and revealed to him what had happened. But if he had hoped to gain further insight into the affair, he was to be disappointed. Manrique had turned pale and was visibly affected, but he merely asked to be granted a few hours leave, departed without a word and was not seen for the rest of the day.

Only at supper did he appear again, but he hardly took any part in the conversation at table, displaying a taciturn gloom, which was unusual for him. In the meantime the ill tidings had spread throughout the garrison and all hesitated between reluctance to

97

touch upon their comrade's trouble and the desire to receive an explanation of this incomprehensible matter, whereby the latter interest understandably began to gain the upper hand. It was Don Jaime who finally overcame his scruples and who asked Manrique directly what in God's name was the truth about this crime, which Manrique's mother was supposed to have committed?

Manrique's expression darkened. Every one was looking at him expectantly, but seconds passed before he finally gave an evasive response: he declared himself not yet sufficiently acquainted with the Doña Leonor was filled with the utmost anxiety. She knew well how facts of the case to make any definite statement concerning it.

There was an embarrassed silence. Nobody dared to change the subject, or to press on with further questions. At last Doña Leonor raised her voice and expressed her conviction that the shameful accusation of murder had been merely invented by the Count de Luna in order to punish the son through his mother. But these words, which had been intended to offer comfort and encouragement to Manrique, only caused his countenance to darken further. He muttered an apology and left the solar, abandoning the company for the rest of the evening.

deeply Manrique loved his mother and she had always felt a certain jealousy towards this woman. When she had accompanied Manrique to Castellar she had thought that they would now be free of all ties with the past. She had believed that he now belonged solely to her as she now belonged solely to him. But here it was again, this past. It lay like a threatening shadow over the protective carapace of their intimacy, and Doña Leonor had to admit to herself that even now Manrique no longer belonged to her alone.

With growing alarm she observed his conduct during the following days and what she perceived was hardly calculated to allay her fears. Manrique would not utter a word concerning his mother, either to her or to Don Jaime; instead he began to consort more frequently with Alfonso Ruiz. Did he wish to confide in his childhood playmate, who was the only one there who knew Azucena? On one occasion Doña Leonor saw the two of them in close conversation with a third man, a soldier whom she knew to be one of Don Jaime's most daring spies and who was apprised of everything that took place in the camp outside. It was he who had recently brought the fateful news of the old woman's arrest. Was Manrique speaking to him of this?

Yet, a little later she found him immersed in the study of a document, so absorbed that he had not noticed her approach. When she addressed him, he gave a start and hastily folded up the document. But she had seen what it contained: a sketch, with arrows and markings. Could it be a plan of the enemy camp? For the love of God, what was Manrique planning? Did he want to steal into the camp – did he plan to liberate his mother in a surprise attack, on his own, without his Commander knowing? That was total madness!

After passing a sleepless night, Doña Leonor resolved to prevail upon him to discuss the matter with her, come what may. Every day that passed might be the last opportunity for her to dissuade him from his foolhardy plan. The next morning she hastened to Manrique's chamber, but did not find him there. She searched for him all over the castle, but he was nowhere to be found. Was it too late – had what she feared taken place that very night? The very thought made her feel faint with fear. In a feverish panic she ran upstairs and down, until at last she espied a lone figure high up on one of the watch towers, and God be praised, it was the one she sought! Doña Leonor climbed up the steps and paused at the top of the platform, breathing heavily. Manrique stood motionless in the biting wind, gazing down at the enemy camp, at the tents, the ditches, the multitude of swarming soldiers. There was no doubt about it: the attack on the castle was imminent.

Doña Leonor, still totally overcome with the anxiety she had felt when searching for him, hurried to his side, and, without more ado, spoke out what she had come to say. 'Manrique', she cried, wringing her hands, 'for the sake of our love, do not do this! Desist from the plan you are contemplating! It will not bring your mother back, it will only drag you down too – and you know that your death would also be mine.'

Manrique, deep in thought, gave a violent start and visibly taken aback and annoyed, turned around to find Doña Leonor standing before him. But at the sight of her there in such a state of feverish agitation, struggling to draw breath and looking into his eyes with such anxious love, his irritation melted away and he was no longer able to deny the intention which she had ascribed to him with such conviction.

'Dearest', he responded, grasping her hands, 'how can you foresee what will happen? If God wills, I will return with my mother. And if I am taken, then at least I will have the consolation that I tried to do what was right.'

'It is not right to court danger senselessly!' Doña Leonor insisted vehemently. 'Look at those men down there, Manrique! All, all of them will stand between you and your mother!'

'In this fortress we are also close to death', replied Manrique, tenderly laying his arm around her trembling shoulders. 'Just see how they are drawing up the canons! Any time now they will sound the attack.'

'Then let them sound the attack! Let them kill all of us!' Doña Leonor exclaimed passionately, and in her eyes there shone defiance of death. 'Then at least we will die together, you and I, side by side!'

She threw himself into his arms and their lips met in a passionate kiss.

'Oh, Leonor', whispered Manrique, overcome by emotion, 'I wish I could live – live with you!'

'Then do not leave me now, Manrique!' Doña Leonor implored him. 'I am your betrothed – with God's help I will soon be your wife! There are still secret ways into the castle – the priest, who is to marry us, may get here any time now...'

She paused as she saw Manrique's expression darken. In order to spare their feelings they had not told the women of the priest's fate.

'Tis true, there are still secret ways', Manrique admitted, as he detached himself from the girl's embrace and once more began to pace the battlements of the castle. 'And I intend to use them before it is too late.'

Doña Leonor shivered in the cool wind. 'Does she mean so

much to you… so much more that I do?' she asked in a subdued voice.

Manrique turned violently. 'She is my mother!' he burst out. 'She will always be, even if it turns out… She cared for me. She brought me up. She taught me all that I know. How can I now abandon her as she lies helpless in a dungeon, sick in body and soul, robbed of all her possessions, branded as a criminal! How can I stand by while people pass judgement over her who have no idea of the true circumstances, or of her state of mind – who see her as nothing more than a cold-blooded child murderer?'

'Manrique, please, tell me the truth!' Doña Leonor begged, timidly drawing near him. 'Did your mother actually do what they are accusing her of? Did she murder the Count's son?'

Manrique hesitated and looked away. He felt that he owed her a clear answer, anxious as she was; and yet he could not possibly tell her of that strange confession Azucena had made to him, of the suspicion that had flashed through his mind, a mystery that troubled him to this day…

'She was without doubt involved in the events at that time', he declared finally, choosing a middle way between candour and restraint, 'only, whatever she may have done, took place under circumstances of extreme emotional pressure when she was in a state of total despair, which threw her mind into confusion, robbing it of all its reason. If what I surmise turns out to be true, she bears a far greater burden of guilt towards herself than before the laws of men. And she expiates this guilt every day, as she lives in remorse and sorrow.'

Doña Leonor was listening to this speech with bated breath, but felt that afterwards she was none the wiser. What did he mean by the phrase 'guilt towards herself'? She opened her lips to ask him, but he raised his hand, asking for silence.

'Ask no more – let that be enough', he requested. 'I cannot tell you any more now, dearest. Wait until my mother is here. She will solve this mystery for us.'

He gently took his beloved's arm and led her down from the tower. 'You will like her – and she will like you', he spoke encouragingly to her. 'She has been guarding this secret for many years.

But now she can no longer keep silent. It could be of the utmost importance, it could change everything, also for the two of us...'

Doña Leonor raised no more objections. His confidence had something infectious about it, and his intimation that there was an important secret to be divulged, did not fail to arouse her curiosity. She still considered his resolve to be foolhardy, and she had failed in her purpose to dissuade him from it. Nevertheless she felt in a strange way calmed and comforted by their talk. Manrique had confided in her. He had trusted her. They had broken through the wall of silence which had threatened to alienate them, and this result alone was sufficient to allay Doña Leonor's fears. Perhaps Manrique was right. Perhaps he really would succeed in snatching his mother from the jaws of death. He was sure to have a good plan. And he had become so brave, so wise, so skilful. If anyone could succeed, it would be he.

IV

Two days later there was a change in the weather: whereas in the preceding days a mild autumn sun had shone from a clear blue sky, now black clouds gathered, bringing cold rain and mist. Manrique could not have wished for anything better for the audacious plan he had in mind and he agreed with Ruiz that they would carry it out the following night. Indeed, there was no time to be lost. Manrique knew that Azucena was to be taken to Zaragoza as soon as she had recovered from her influenza. Any day now she could disappear beyond his reach.

The two friends waited until the last sounds had died down in the enemy camp. Then they silently left the protection of the castle. They did not use either of the two gates which were heavily guarded, both from within and without, but climbed down the back wall using rope ladders. Unseen, they reached the perimeter of the camp and tiptoed towards its outer defences.

The house in which Azucena was held captive, was a side wing of the farm that the Count de Luna used as his headquarters. Although it was some distance from the soldiers' tents, strong guards had been posted near it, so that if need be the entire camp could be alarmed within seconds. They had to be immobilized, and without a sound – everything depended on this. Even the slightest sound could ruin the whole enterprise. It was totally dark, but from his vantage point on the watch tower Manrique had worked out a route that he thought might be feasible; he had carefully memorised all its hidden dangers and distinguishing features. There was only one soldier on patrol there. It would not be difficult to slip past him, and then the way through the camp would be free.

Manrique led the way, with Ruiz following, flitting like a sha-dow, here leaping over a trench, there negotiating a way round an obstacle. They reached the tents without incident and with bated breath now approached their goal, the Commander's head-quarters. From the watch tower Manrique had not been able to see this part of their route; he could envisage it only through des-criptions and sketches. But as he approached he was guided by a faint ray of light which illuminated the guard room of the camp.

All of a sudden two figures materialised out of the darkness a short way from them – soldiers who were patrolling round the farm. Manrique and Alfonso Ruiz swiftly hid themselves behind a tree. With beating hearts they watched as the guards walked past, barely five paces away from them, and disappeared into the mist. What a good thing that the night was so dark! They could not have chosen a better one.

Now all they had to do was to overcome the sentries outside the guardhouse. No one could get past them without being seen. In the shadow of the house wall the attackers crept as close to them as possible, and at a sign from Manrique both sprang simul-taneously into the circle of light. Before the sentries had time to recover from their surprise and sound the alarm they had been felled silently to the ground. Manrique did not want any blood to be shed on this mission, which concerned only him and his mo-ther. The sentries were merely tied together and their mouths stuffed with tow. Then Manrique and Alfonso Ruiz hastened to-wards the side building in which Azucena was held captive.

They found the front door unlocked and groped their way along a dark passage. Manrique knew from his informant that Azucena was kept locked in the cellar and that one of the Count de Luna's servants had been assigned to act both as her guard and medical attendant. Unfortunately his informant had been unable to tell them anything about the layout of the house, so that the two friends had to spend valuable minutes feeling their way until they finally discovered the door leading into the cellar. But as they descended the spiral staircase another source of light appeared before them. It came from an oil lamp that stood on the table in the guard room at the bottom of the stairs; beside it was a plate with remnants of food, and an empty carafe of wine. And behind this table, in a capacious armchair, they espied Azucena's guard, a small, fat man with a bunch of keys on his belt. His head had sunk back against the chair and he was breathing heavily, in a peaceful slumber.

The friends exchanged a look of relief. This was the moment that had caused them their greatest headache when planning the enterprise: the moment they would have to get close to the guard who was best placed to see them coming and to sound the alarm. Using hand signals they agreed to tie the man directly to the armchair; and indeed, he only woke up when the cords were drawn around his shoulders. With a final snort of shock he started up, but at once had a handful of tow stuffed into his mouth; and while Alfonso rapidly finished tying up the man, Manrique was already removing the keys from his belt.

It was the work of a moment to open the iron-barred gate which led to several cells separated from each other by rough wooden doors – but which of them contained the prisoner? Valuable seconds were lost while he tried to find the right key. In the first cell there was nothing but tools, but when Manrique opened the second, he found to his joy the one he sought. She was lying on a bed of straw, semi-conscious, in that restless half sleep of the sick. Her hair was tousled, her face emaciated.

Manrique shook her by the shoulder, calling to her in a soft voice. Azucena turned her head aside and muttered in a surly voice, clearly immersed in a dream which she was not able to shake off. Manrique shook her more violently.

'Mother', he cried again, 'it is I, Manrique!'

At last his voice penetrated her consciousness. She gave a start, opened her eyes wide and saw Manrique standing beside her bed. She was about to give a cry of shock, but he swiftly pressed his hand to her mouth.

'Quiet. Don't make a sound, Mother', he whispered. 'Get up and put on your cloak, we are taking you to Castellar.'

He took his hand from her mouth, but Azucena had not yet overcome her astonishment.

'Manrique!' she breathed, overcome by emotion. 'You here, in this place of death!? But no, it must be a dream. They would never allow you to come to me...'

'Mother!' Manrique was becoming impatient. 'Wake up! It isn't a dream! I have come to set you free!'

'You are here! You have come to set me free!' Azucena repeated with a joyful smile. 'Oh, yes, a beautiful dream at last... not like the other, tormenting ones...'

Manrique began to break out into sweat. He had known that his mother was ill, but had not realized how powerfully the illness had affected her reason.

'You will set me free, and we will go home', Azucena spoke in a delirium, now totally caught up in a blissful delusion. 'We will go back to our village... How happy we were there, Manrique! In the evenings I taught you to play the lute... you were such a sweet, gifted child...'

Manrique seized her by the shoulders and tried to pull her up from the bed. 'Mother!' he cried in despair. 'Get up. Do get up! Every second is precious! We must get away from here with the utmost speed!'

'No, don't wake me – let me dream a little longer, Manrique', Azucena murmured, trying to evade his grasp. 'I will be leaving here soon enough... far away into death, where they can no longer torment me.'

'Manrique', Alfonso Ruiz now intervened, having heard every word from the guard room. 'You see that she cannot understand anything! We must leave her here, it is pointless!'

'But before that they shall hear the truth', Azucena continued, with a far away expression. 'When they drag me before their court, I will shout it out for all to hear…The judge will have pity on me… The highest judge, up there in heaven…'

Devastated, Manrique stood before her. His reason told him that Alfonso was right, but his heart would not let him believe that all their efforts had been in vain, that his mother was lost to him. What was he to do, seize her by force, carry her out of the dungeon against her will?

Ruiz hastened through the iron-barred gate. 'Manrique', he urged, 'do come on! Any moment now the guard could be changed!' But his departure from the guardroom was to prove fatal. Although Azucena's guard had been tied to the chair from head to hips, his legs had been left free, and as soon as he knew that he was alone in the room, he drew them up and used them to push himself away from the table, with a strength that was surprising in one of his girth. This caused a loud thump and a crash, which sounded like thunder in the stillness of the night. The table toppled over, the plates smashed, the oil lamp broke in two with a deafening clatter and the oil poured out from it, the burning wick catching it alight, so that in a flash the whole pool of oil had gone up in flames.

'Curses!' hissed Ruiz. 'Come away, at once!'

Meanwhile Azucena, alarmed by the noise, had sprung up from the bed and was staring in horror at the guardroom where the flames were leaping, higher and higher.

'The fire… Oh, I knew it would come again' she muttered, clutching her head with both hands. 'It keeps coming back…It will never end…'

'Give me your hand, mother!' Manrique cried. 'I'm taking you with me whether you will or no!'

'Are you as mad as she is?' Ruiz hissed at him. 'Do you want to destroy us too? You can no longer help her, so let us leave now, before it is too late!'

They could already hear shouts from without, steps were hastening towards them, lanterns were being lit. Azucena, rigid with terror, had retreated to the back of her cell and was pointing at the flames with an outstretched arm.

'The time has come!' she cried. 'They are coming to fetch me! They will burn me, just as they did my mother...'

The two friends ran out into the guardroom, where they tore off their jackets and with powerful blows put out the flames. Then they sprang up the cellar stairs and hastened out into the open. But no sooner had they reached the courtyard, which was now brightly illuminated with flaming torches and lanterns, than they found their way barred by soldiers. They rushed back into the house, blocked the entrance and escaped out of the back window. But even the back of the house was now illuminated by torches. Armed men, some only half clad, hastened towards them, cutting off every means of escape. They soon found themselves surrounded by superior numbers, which were growing by the minute. Alfonso, in the desperate hope of making a breach for himself and his friend, struck down one of their attackers, but when he attempted to break through the circle of soldiers one of them plunged his sword into Alfonso's back, and Manrique, now overpowered and held by four men, was forced to look on helplessly as his friend expired at his feet.

Meanwhile the Count de Luna appeared at the door of his quarters, still dazed with sleep, his cloak hastily thrown over his nightgown. He was told of what had happened, and Manrique was led before him. The Count was almost speechless with amazement and triumph as he looked into the eyes of his rival. How remarkably, but also how meaningfully, did providence reign over him! The arrest of a half mad woman, ordered by mistake, not only delivered up to him the murderer of his brother, but through her the man who had besmirched his own honour.

An officer, saluting, asked what should be done with the prisoner. Don Nuño opened his mouth several times to speak before he was able to answer, and when he spoke at last, his voice sounded hollow.

'This man has come to see his mother', said he, pointing at Manrique, who, with an expression of deepest suffering, held his rival's mocking gaze. 'He may share the cellar with her! As soon as possible I will have the two of them taken to Zaragoza.'

V

The Count d'Urgell was beside himself when he heard the news the following morning of what had happened. Ruiz dead! Manrique Corda taken prisoner! Both the victims of an illicit, private venture that had been carried out, in flagrant disregard of every rule of military conduct, indeed, contrary to all ordinary human reason! Don Jaime hardly knew whether he should weep for Manrique or curse him for committing a crime. He would have given much if he could have torn the captain, who was as dear to him as a son, from the clutches of the enemy – and then to have punished him most severely.

But there was not the slightest prospect of his being able to do either the one or the other. The Count de Luna, once he had heard the details of the nocturnal adventure, entertained the gravest anxiety lest Manrique should manage to escape from his imprisonment – after all, he had already shown what bold manoeuvres he was capable of – or that there could be an attempt by the castle forces to liberate him. Thus Don Nuño issued orders that the prisoners be conveyed, under heavy guard, to Zaragoza, that very day. In vain did the regiment's doctor warn him that the sick woman might not survive the journey. Don Nuño, faced with the two alternatives, which both posed a risk, chose to see her dead rather than free.

He gave order that preparations for the transport of the prisoners be made at a place that would be clearly visible from the towers of the fortress, for it was his wish that those confined within – amongst whom there was one person in particular that he had in mind - should learn at once of his action. When the Count d'Urgell was informed that preparations were being made in the camp for the transport of Manrique Corda and his mother in a closed wagon, the Commander went in person to the watch tower, followed by his wife, who was equally concerned about Manrique's fate.

Once they had reached the battlements the two discovered that they were not the first to climb to the tower. Doña Leonor, as soon as she received the news that Manrique had been captured, had, with shaking knees, climbed up the stairs leading to the same watch tower where, only a few days before, she had implored her betrothed to give up his plan; and it was here that she now stood alone on the parapet, her gaze directed unwaveringly at the enemy camp below.

In silence Don Jaime and Doña Isabel joined her on the parapet. It was not possible to see far from this distance, especially as the weather was dull and misty. Dimly they could discern behind the encampment the covered wagon which was to transport the prisoners to Zaragoza. Soldiers were busy harnessing horses to it and loading up the baggage. It appeared that within the wagon a special cage was being constructed for the sick woman, lined with straw. Standing apart were some officers, presumably watching over the work. Doña Leonor thought she could recognize one of them as the Count de Luna; the d'Urgells had never before set eyes on him.

Finally the prisoners were led out. Azucena was too weak to walk unaided. Supported and almost carried by her guards she climbed into the wagon with great difficulty and was placed in the cage. Then Manrique appeared between two soldiers, who held him by the arms. It was hard to discern his figure, although Doña Leonor leaned dangerously far over the parapet. She could however see clearly how the Count de Luna – it was certainly he, the man she hated! – stepped forth from the group of officers and stopped in front of his prisoner. What could the victor be saying to the one he had vanquished? Was he adding mockery to his triumph?

Now it was Manrique who climbed into the wagon. For a moment his guards loosened their grip on him, and he used the moment to turn his head suddenly towards the castle and to lift his arm as if in a greeting. It would have been impossible for him to have recognized the three figures in the watch tower of the castle. And yet it gave them the illusion that he knew them to be there, that he was looking directly up at them and offering them his greeting of farewell.

The Count and the Countess d'Urgell cast a surreptitious glance at Doña Leonor and saw that she also had raised her arm in a greeting. Her lips were moving as if in prayer. But it was no prayer that her lips were forming. It was a solemn promise, borne silently by the wind across the space separating them to her beloved who now disappeared into the wagon.

The soldiers who were guarding them had clearly been ordered to set off and swung themselves onto their horses. The driver loosed the reins and the wagon, escorted by the riders, moved slowly away. The three people watching from the tower were able to follow its progress for a while, as the track led up a hill. Don Jaime, at the sight of the wagon disappearing into the distance, felt his resentment of Manrique melt away. It was replaced by a sense of helplessness and grief, and his heart was filled with a deep pity as he contemplated the ill fortune that had dogged this man's life. So richly endowed by nature, so obviously predestined for a superior position in the world – what was it that kept driving him to fight for the underdog, for the defeated Commander, for the deranged woman, and to endanger his own life for such as these?

When the wagon disappeared over the brow of the hill, Doña Leonor, now losing all self control, sank to the floor of the parapet, sobbing loudly. The Countess tried to lead her away, but she refused to budge from the spot. The d'Urgells finally decided that it would be best to leave her alone and they quietly withdrew from the tower.

But one hour after another passed, without Doña Leonor being seen by her friends. When the time for supper approached Doña Isabel became seriously concerned. Up there on the tower the evening wind was cutting, and Doña Leonor's health had already suffered. So the Countess climbed up the stairs once more, resolved to bring her friend to reason.

But she had not climbed very far when a shadow fell on the stair above and the person she sought came down towards her of her own accord. She was no longer weeping now, and her expression was that of one who had reached a bitter, but unavoidable decision.

'I thank you for coming, Countess', said she in a firm voice. 'I was just going to find you. May I speak with you in private? It is about a matter of the utmost importance to me.'

The Countess, who was secretly astonished at this change in her friend's conduct, suggested her closet as the best place in which to hold a discussion undisturbed. Thither the two ladies repaired, and there they remained for several hours, deaf to all entreaties from the outside world. Not a single soul would ever learn what passed between Doña Leonor and her friend at this fateful hour. For the rest of her life the Countess refused to reveal any information concerning this time, to anyone, even to her husband. One servant, however, thought he heard the Countess trying desperately to dissuade Doña Leonor from something; but she seemed to be unable to prevail against the young girl's resolve.

At last the door was pushed open and Doña Isabel appeared with a key in her hand. Normally so brave, this woman now had hot tears running down her cheeks. She hastened, followed by Doña Leonor, to a small chamber that was near by, and disappeared within. When she came out she was holding in her hand a small green crystal flask, which she handed to her friend.

'There! Take it in God's name!' she spoke in a trembling voice. 'But only as a last resort, do you hear? This poison is not to be trifled with. It takes about a quarter of an hour until it achieves its full effect, but then death comes immediately... Ah! That this should be my parting gift to you!'

Doña Leonor tried to embrace her in a surge of gratitude, but the Countess tore herself away and fled, sobbing, to her chamber.

VI

About an hour later, when the evening was already far advanced, the officer on duty for the night watch asked to speak to Count de Luna in his quarters. His manner denoted great astonishment and embarrassment, as though he had experienced something quite remarkable; and certainly, what he related to the Count was indeed remarkable: a female person had just appeared in front of his soldiers. Apparently she had come from the fortress, but no one could say how she had contrived to leave it. She had walked right up to the sentries and had declared that she must speak to Count de Luna urgently, this instant. In response to the question as to her name, she had given one of the nobility: Leonor de Sesé, if he could…

Don Nuño sprang up and ordered them to bring the lady to him at once. A few minutes later Doña Leonor, flanked by two of the guards, entered the room. She was clad in a black cloak and carried in her hand a bundle. The Count had meanwhile gathered his wits and received her sitting at his desk, with the cool, dignified manner befitting a Commander.

'What a surprise', said he nonchalantly, in a casual tone, motioning to the guards that they should withdraw.

Doña Leonor was unable to respond to this, so that seconds passed in silence, with nothing to be heard but the crackling of the fire. Finally Don Nuño spoke again, and asked, this time in a more severe tone, to what did he owe the honour of her visit. At that Doña Leonor, overcome by emotion, rushed towards him and threw herself at his feet, with such violence that her cloak fell from her shoulders.

'Mercy, my Lord!' she gasped, in a half whisper. 'If I was ever dear to you…'

Don Nuño felt moved, and the expression of severity he had assumed, melted away. That she should implore his forgiveness was more than he had expected. How pale and exhausted she looked – and yet, how well this pallor became her! Gently he raised her to her feet and placed her in his own chair, while he himself sat down on a stool, took her hand and declared with passion that she was still infinitely dear to him – dearer than all the world! Nothing, he assured her, had ever shaken his love for her, not even the lamentable aberration to which she had succumbed, and now that she had fortunately put this behind her, he would gladly forgive her.

Doña Leonor tore her hand away and stared at him as if at a madman. 'But – I do not want anything for myself!' she cried. 'Punish me, as severely as you wish, but spare Manrique!'

The Count understood, and his disillusionment brought in its wake a cold fury. So that was it! She was visiting him in the hope of saving the wretched life of her paramour! She held him to be such a fool that she thought he might forego his triumph over his rival on account of her tears and her languishing eyes! On the contrary, my beautiful supplicant! I will crush him to smithereens! He stood up and said, looking coolly down on her, that she would do better never to utter the name of the wretch in his hearing again. Doña Leonor looked up at him imploringly, but then lowered her eyes in discouragement. In his look she had read nothing but inexorable mercilessness.

'Mercy, my Lord?', she repeated helplessly.

'Get out!' cried Don Nuño, overcome with rage. 'Just because of your pleading, the churl shall suffer torture ten times over!'

Doña Leonor wrung her hands. 'Take me in his place!' she begged. 'I am willing to suffer torture a hundred times over. I am willing to die the cruellest of deaths! I am the guilty one, I followed him! No other should suffer for what I have done!'

Don Nuño stamped his foot. 'Must I have you thrown out by the guards?'

With a look of defeat in her eyes Doña Leonor stood up. The Count picked up her cloak and held it out to her in a commanding gesture. She, however, now hesitated, still desperately searching for a way out.

'If you let Manrique go...' she stammered. 'I would be willing to pay any price...'

'Enough!' cried Don Nuño impatiently. 'There is no price that could buy his freedom!'

'But supposing...I would... offer myself...?'

Her lips uttered the two last words almost imperceptibly. Don Nuño hesitated, looking searchingly at her. There was a glowing tension in her expression. She resembled a gambler playing his last trump card.

'You said just now that you still love me', she spoke with a trembling voice. 'That you could forgive me, for... succumbing to a lamentable aberration, as you put it. Now I take you at your word: the moment you set Manrique Corda free, I will be yours!'

Don Nuño let her cloak fall. So it had come to this: the honour he had once offered to her was now being offered to him in the form of a sacrifice. My God, how she must love this scoundrel! He must be destroyed, absolutely, it was impossible to let him go on living... And yet, would not this be a true death for him: to remain alive, only to witness his own utter failure? If he were to be robbed of all that was dear to him, his mother, the woman he loved, his Commander, everything, and if he were made to experience each one of these losses consciously and painfully? Oh yes, he would be made to watch Castellar being razed to the ground, to watch as his mother, that evil witch, was burned at the stake, and then, the ultimate torture, to watch Doña Leonor becoming Countess de Luna! No triumph could be more perfect!

But how long could he be sure of this triumph? If Manrique Corda remained alive, it might still be possible for him to approach Doña Leonor once more – and could he then still be sure of her? Whatever promise she made to him now, she would break it for the sake of the other man. No, no, he had to die, what she was demanding could not be fulfilled...

And yet, what was her actual demand? That her lover be set free – well, that could easily be arranged. Of course, careful note would have to be taken of the direction he took, but after a few weeks, once Doña Leonor was Countess de Luna and safely protected, should a fatal accident befall him in the mountains, this could not constitute a breach of promise – she did not even need to learn of it.

The Count took Doña Leonor by the shoulders, forcing her to look him in the eye. 'You will be mine for ever?' he asked, roughly.

'I swear it, my Lord.' Her words were barely a whisper, but her burning look held his.

'You are not planning to trick me?'

Doña Leonor lowered her eyes briefly, but then looked up at him again with an expression of determination. 'As soon as you set Manrique free, I will be yours unto death!'

Don Nuño turned away and paced to and fro for a while, contemplating. At last he stopped once more in front of Doña Leonor. 'For the time being you will take up quarters in the village', he instructed her, in a commanding tone. 'One of the peasant girls may serve you.'

'I am yours to command, Count', answered Doña Leonor, with a slight bow.

'As soon as I can get away from here, we will travel together to Zaragoza. There I will fulfil my part of the bargain, and then you will fulfil yours. The marriage will take place in Zaragoza, quietly, without guests, without causing any attention. The actual wedding celebration will take place a few weeks later in my Castillo. It will be the most magnificent affair ever to be seen in this country.'

With a faint smile Doña Leonor waved this away, as if the celebration was the last of her concerns. But this smile alone gave Don Nuño the courage to step closer to her. Impulsively he wrapped his arms around her slender hips.

'One day you will be happy' he assured her, now in a softer tone. 'As soon as you have become used...'

'I will be happy, certainly', she interrupted him, detaching herself from his embrace with a slight shudder, 'as soon as I know that Manrique has been saved.'

Don Nuño called the guards and issued orders that a wagon be harnessed immediately and the lady conveyed to the village. She was to be provided with every comfort, her every wish fulfilled and the peasants instructed to treat her with the greatest respect and obedience – as she was the betrothed of the Count de Luna!

VII

The following day the attack on the fortress began, much earlier than had been expected, and to the total surprise, not only of the besieged garrison, but also of the besieging troops, for until this point their Commander had prepared for this final stage with great thoroughness and caution. This approach was in accordance with the instructions given to him by the King, who did not want the early part of his reign to be besmirched by blood and who put the safety of his troops above all other considerations. Now, however, Don Nuño declared that the encirclement of the castle was complete and that the element of surprise would be an immeasurable tactical advantage. Brushing aside his officers' objections, he ordered the attack, throwing all his regiments into the battle, even calling upon the reservists from surrounding towns to come thither with all speed. His ultimate victory was of course beyond doubt – the superior strength of the forces at his command was all too great. But the soldiers under siege put up a furious resistance and caused the Royal army many losses which could certainly have been avoided if a more cautious approach had been adopted. The Count d'Urgell and his valiant men held Castellar for two whole weeks, which was far longer than had been expected. But in the end they were forced to yield to the superior numbers of their enemies and the Royal troops marched triumphantly into the castle.

This was the moment that Don Nuño had been awaiting with impatience. He declared to the assembled officers that it was now his duty to inform the King personally that his mission had been accomplished and that in consequence the war of succession, which had drained the resources of the land for two whole years, was at an end. He intended therefore to travel to Zaragoza the very next day. He left the command in the hands of the highest ranking officer and sent word to his bride that she should make herself ready to travel early the following morning.

During these two weeks in the village below, where the Count had provided her with lodgings, day after day Doña Leonor had heard the thunder of the cannons, and the roar of battle. When at last silence fell, she knew what this signified, and she was filled with sorrow as she thought of the vanquished up there in the fortress, whose lives she had shared over many weeks. However, at the same time, her heart beat faster with mingled feelings of hope and fear, in anticipation of the crucial events that lay ahead: now Manrique's destiny would be fulfilled, and thus hers also.

Fortunately the Count de Luna was so heavily occupied and over burdened during the storming of Castellar that he seldom had time to visit her. She had impressed upon her lady's maid, who was a sensible peasant girl, that she should not leave the room for a moment when the Count was present, for even his slightest touch filled her with revulsion, as if it sullied her body.

The mere fact that she had to allow herself to be referred to as the Count's bride was a constant insult to her spirit. Frequently, when she was alone, she pulled forth the little green flask from her bosom, where she always kept it hidden, and felt a sweet feeling of consolation at the thought of the freedom it promised.

Early on the appointed day, the Count sent a carriage to the village, which was to bring her to him in the fortress. He could have fetched her from the village himself, as it lay directly on the route to Zaragoza, but his masculine pride demanded that he show off to the world the beautiful conquest he had wrested from the enemy. Thus it came about that Doña Leonor was forced to enter once more the place where, in the midst of warfare, she had experienced a time of love and happiness. It was through this gate that she had entered the castle, by Manrique's side. Behind the window up there was the solar where Manrique was wont to sing of an evening – how the sound of his voice still rang in her ears! And the staircase there led up to the watch tower from where she had watched him depart.

Now of course she felt estranged in this place, once so familiar to her, but now savagely laid waste by cannon fire and the excesses of the victorious troops. Don Jaime and his wife had been placed under arrest and were held under heavy guard until the King passed judgement upon them. Of his men about two hundred had survived the storming of the fortress and these were now confined as prisoners in its cellars and dungeons. As Doña Leonor stepped out of the carriage, a group of them was being led in chains into the courtyard. These men, for whom there was no more room in the cellar, were to be taken to various prisons in the surrounding district, where they were likewise to await the King's verdict. Doña Leonor watched them as one after the other, they stepped out of the cellar door into the open, blinking in the unaccustomed daylight, some stumbling in the chains with which they were closely linked together. How emaciated they all looked, how exhausted and defeated! How hard their struggle must have been, which had ultimately ended in this bitter defeat! They had kept faith with their Commander and now they would be made to pay the penalty for doing so. What fate awaited them?

Many passed by apathetically, paying no heed to their surroundings. But some looked across at Doña Leonor and she could not but notice the expression of bitter contempt in their faces. All these men had known her as the bride of Manrique Corda. And now she was standing here as the bride of the victor. At once Don Nuño, clad in gala uniform, hastened towards her, greeted her and gallantly offered her his arm. With satisfaction he observed that beneath her cloak she was wearing a white dress, certainly in preparation for their approaching nuptials. The guards and officers standing nearby, most of whom had not set eyes on a woman for several weeks, stared at her with lust in their eyes as she walked towards the castle at the side of the Count, and she was powerless to defend herself, in the hateful role she had to play. She cast a final glance at the prisoners in the courtyard before the door shut behind her. They would never know that they had been wrong about her – that her destiny lay not with this smiling victor, but solely with death. Nestling in her bosom she could feel the Countess d'Urgell's little green flask, warm and consoling. Soon she would find redemption and be cleansed of all this, forever.

Zaragoza was a good day's journey away. The Count de Luna travelled with his bride through the countryside in a carriage and four, followed by servants and soldiers on horseback, as was fitting for a gentleman in his position. At midday they stopped at an inn and then, fortified, they continued their journey. Doña Leonor, for whom their close proximity in the confined and darkened space within the carriage was a constant torture, had withdrawn as far as possible into the furthest corner, under the pretext of wishing to rest; but she responded politely when the Count addressed her, as for instance when he pointed out to her some detail in the landscape. Only when the towers of Zaragoza became visible in the distance did she direct their conversation to the ultimate aim of their journey by asking the Count when he intended to set Manrique free.

'If all goes well, this very evening', answered Don Nuño, promptly and decisively, for he had in the meantime been planning in his mind the course of events down to the minutest detail. 'And immediately afterwards we will be married in San Martin. I

gave the priest there the relevant instructions a week ago. He will
be expecting us any time.'

'This very evening!' Doña Leonor repeated, and a barely per-
ceptible pallor passed over her face, like a breath of death. But in
a moment she had composed herself and spoke with calm cour-
tesy: 'Just as you wish, Count.'

Indeed, it suited the Count very well if the prisoner were to be
set free, not in broad daylight, but at night time. Manrique Corda
was being held, as was his mother, in a tower within the Aljafería,
which was kept under close surveillance. To be sure, Don Nuño
could enter at any time, and was in charge of the guards, but as
the King and his family were staying in the immediate vicinity,
during the day there would have been a danger that he, or one of
the infantas, might have noticed the enemy of the state being set
free, and asked the reason for it. It would be difficult enough for
Don Nuño to provide his strict sovereign after the event with even
a half plausible explanation, although it would surely be possible
to come up with one. At any rate, a fait accompli seemed to him
the safest option. In his heart he felt something whisper that the
bargain he had struck with Doña Leonor was not to be trusted,
that she could revoke it at any time. It was for this reason that he
had pressed on with the conquest of Castellar, regardless of the
losses sustained, and it was for this reason that he was now in
such haste to have Manrique Corda set free and to have the marriage carried out immediately afterwards. He would find no peace
until Doña Leonor had become his wife before God and the world.

VIII

The great square tower, in which Manrique Corda lay confined,
was situated by the outer wall of the Aljafería, away from the
bustle of the palace but yet close enough to attract the attention
of the inhabitants. Many of them still remembered the singing
tournament when the prisoner had touched all their hearts with
his voice; and sometimes at twilight, when all the noise of the day
had died away, his voice could be heard once more, resounding

through the walls, faintly, yet still with that wonderful tone and deep feeling: 'Time and space were lost to me, I saw you in eternity...'

Then they paused to listen on their patios and in their chambers, the court ladies and the caballeros, the pages, the lady's maids, and the soldiers on guard, who all inhabited the palace. The ladies in particular were enchanted by his singing, and they thronged to the tower so that they could listen more closely. Even outside the walls a small crowd of listeners was often to be observed and the tale of the unhappy singer, cast into the dungeon by cruel fate, was passed from mouth to mouth. Still today this part of the Aljafería is referred to as the 'Tower of the Troubadour'.

However, on the evening when the Count de Luna entered the court and approached the tower, accompanied by his bride, all clad in white, and followed by his escort, the bell had already tolled eleven and all sounds had died away. The palace lay silent, as if deserted; only a few night torches cast a flickering light over the sombre scene. In response to the Count's knock, a sleepy captain of the guard peered out of the window, only to withdraw abruptly in astonishment at the unexpected invasion. He led the pair into a bare chamber, while the men who were escorting the Count awaited his orders outside in the courtyard.

The Count gave his directions in a firm voice. He demanded the keys from the captain, explaining that he wished to visit the prisoner Manrique Corda. The captain meanwhile was to run across to the chapel of San Martin – it was also situated close by the outer wall, just one courtyard away from the tower – and to rouse the priest from his chamber. A marriage ceremony was to be performed, the priest already knew all about it.

The captain handed over the keys to the Count, saluted, and hastened away. The Count turned to Doña Leonor and bade her stand at the window. From there, he explained, she could see for herself that he was fulfilling his side of the bargain. She could even, if she so wished, say a final farewell to him. Of course, Manrique would not be alone. Two men would have to accompany him to the main gate, to ensure that he would be allowed to pass out from there. Then he would be free to go wherever his fancy took him; and should she wish to convince herself of that as well, she was at liberty to climb to the top of the wall – there was a vantage point close by the chapel – and watch him leave.

Doña Leonor indicated her agreement. Little did she suspect that one of the men who were to bring Manrique to the gate, had been given orders by the Count to follow Corda unobtrusively and to provide a detailed account of his whereabouts. She remained behind in the chamber, standing at the window, her hands folded as if she were in prayer. Meanwhile the Count ran out into the courtyard and beckoned to two men in his escort. One of them held the torch, while the other unlocked the door which led up into the tower and the cells. The three then climbed the stairs and emerged into a dark passage. On their right was a door leading to the cell in which Azucena, still feverish, was tossing and turning on her straw pallet. But Manrique was housed in a cell at the furthest end of the corridor, as far away from his mother as possible.

One of the soldiers unlocked the door of Manrique's cell for the Count. The other held the torch aloft, illuminating the chamber within. Manrique was fast asleep on his pallet. Only when the glow of the torch fell upon his face did he wake, blinking in the light. Recognizing the features of the Count, he started up in shock. Was this the harbinger of his approaching death?

Don Nuño stood before him in the wavering light of the torch, his head held high. 'You are free to go', he said, in a tone of contempt, 'this door is open to you. Doña Leonor de Sesé, who will marry me this very night, has secured this act of mercy for you. Take yourself back to your miserable village and never come into my sight, or that of my wife, ever again!'

For several seconds he gazed at his rival, savouring the look of total disbelief and bewilderment as it spread across his face. Then the Count turned away, ordering the soldiers to accompany Corda to the gate, and strode out of the cell. When he passed Azucena's cell he was able to see in the gloom a figure standing at the bars.

'What is happening here?' he heard Azucena's voice. 'Manrique! Can you hear me, my son?'

The Count strode on, paying no heed to her. That brief feeling of triumph had at once been succeeded by a strong sensation of disquiet, impelling him not to leave Doña Leonor alone for too long – as if she could still flee from him, or foil his plans in some way or another. As certain as victory seemed to him, he had not yet won it!

His presentiment was not unfounded: as soon as Doña Leonor found herself alone, she drew her beloved little green flask once more from her bosom. Was it now the moment to use it? Or would it be better to wait until she was certain that Manrique was a free man? He must be far away when she died, for the Count would surely pursue him in his wrath as soon as he realized he had been cheated of his reward.

Yet on the other hand, would she ever have such an opportunity again? She sensed that the Count did not fully trust her. During the entire journey he had not let her out of his sight for a moment, he had followed and watched her every step with a look of suspicion. What if he managed to thwart her purpose – if he took the precious little flask from her, her sole weapon, her sole friend – if she no longer had anything with which to defend herself from his will… Her hand gripped the flask tightly. What had the Countess d'Urgell said exactly? It takes about a quarter of an hour until it achieves its full effect, but then death comes immediately… So she would have a quarter of an hour. Would that not be enough time, whatever the case? She would climb up to that vantage point of which the Count had spoken, and if from there her last sight would be of Manrique striding out to freedom, with what joy she would leave this world…

Suddenly she heard a sound outside in the courtyard. She looked up and saw a dark figure stepping out of the door which led to the prison. It was he, Manrique, it was truly he! The Count had kept his word! Now she should not tarry any longer. An unguarded moment such as this might not come again; and by the time the poison had taken its full effect, Manrique would be far away. Resolutely she pulled off the stopper of the flask and swallowed the contents.

Hardly had she lowered it from her lips when the door behind her opened and the Count de Luna entered the chamber. 'What is the matter with you?' he asked, immediately becoming suspicious. "What is that in your hand?'

But Doña Leonor did not hear him. She stared at him, thunderstruck, and looked out at the desolate courtyard, all in darkness, as if she expected to see someone else there. On her face was an expression of total shock. Could two men resemble each other so closely?

'And... Manrique?' she stammered.

'You need not have no fear, he has already been released', replied Don Nuño contemptuously. 'He will be in the courtyard any moment now.'

Doña Leonor struggled to draw breath. With growing anxiety she kept watch out of the window, yet he, whom she longed to see, did not appear. Her manner struck the Count as increasingly strange.

'What ails you?' he repeated, with growing impatience. 'For God's sake, calm yourself!'

But Doña Leonor was far from calming herself. 'But where is he then?' she cried. 'Why does he not come?'

The Count looked at her with growing suspicion. For the second time he asked: 'What is that you are holding in your hand?'

Doña Leonor tore her eyes from the window and glanced at the flask, which she was still holding tightly in her hand, but had clearly totally forgotten.

'Oh, my...smelling salts', she replied, forcing a smile. 'For a moment I did not feel well.'

She threw the flask carelessly to the floor and once more stared out into the courtyard. Still no one appeared and minutes passed. At last steps were heard, but they came from the opposite direction: the captain, who had been sent to inform the priest, entered and reported to the Count that over in the church all had been made ready for the nocturnal wedding service.

Doña Leonor's whole body began to tremble. 'You have deceived me!' she cried. 'You never intended to set Manrique free!'

Now it was Don Nuño who became nervous and he asked himself what was keeping Manrique.

'He'll still be speaking to his mother', he surmised. 'Wait here, I'll go and see.'

But Doña Leonor, filled with the indignation of one who has been deceived, had not the slightest intention of waiting and followed the Count out into the courtyard. He had just reached the door leading to the prison when it was opened and one of the soldiers who had been ordered to accompany Manrique appeared on the threshold and reported, with a look of puzzlement, that the prisoner was stubbornly refusing to leave his cell. In vain had they urged him not to reject the Count's offer of clemency. The only answer the prisoner would give, was that he would not leave until a particular lady – he named her as Leonor de Sesé – had confirmed to him in person the Count's claim, namely that she was willing to become his wife.

Doña Leonor let out a cry, pushed past the two men and, before anyone could stop her, ran through the door and up the stairs that led to the cells of the prisoners. When she had reached the passage she stood, breathing heavily, and listened anxiously to her heart. How much time did she have left? Three minutes – five minutes? To her right she could discern the figure of a woman. It was Azucena, pressing herself anxiously against the bars of the cell. She had hardly been able to understand anything of what was happening to Manrique, but her mother's heart had a premonition of disaster.

'Please fetch the Count de Luna, at once!' she cried imploringly to Doña Leonor. 'I have something to tell him which will change his mind!'

Doña Leonor was about to approach her, but at that moment she saw Manrique's cell, saw the soldier holding the torch and saw Manrique himself, sitting on his straw pallet, his head bowed. He looked pale, with an expression of suffering, as that of someone who has just received a mortal blow, and yet the mere sight of him filled her with a feeling of glowing happiness. Her heart's wish was about to be fulfilled: the last thing she would see on earth would be the face of her beloved, and if enough time remained for her to speak, she would still be able to save him with her sacrifice!

She hastened to the cell, where the soldier saluted her and made way for her to pass. 'Manrique!' she cried, throwing herself down before him. 'Dearest, it is I, Leonor!'

He raised his head and glanced at her with a look, not of joy at seeing her again but with an expression of bitter hurt.

'Manrique, listen to me', she continued, with breathless haste. 'You must leave – this instant – I have...'

'Just tell me one thing', he interrupted in a hard tone. 'Have you agreed to marry the Count?'

Doña Leonor felt a sudden feeling of weakness in her limbs. Was that just her agitation, or...?

She clasped his knees imploringly. 'Manrique', she spoke in a fearful voice, 'we have no more time! What I agreed with the Count means nothing now! Soon you will understand everything, but go now! Go far away from here, before it is too late! When the Count discovers what I have...'

'Manrique!' they heard Azucena's voice. "For the love of God, answer me! If he intends to kill you, the accursed man – I know the means to save you!'

But Manrique paid no heed to his mother. In horror he was looking down at Doña Leonor, who lay swooning at his feet.

'So it is true', he said. 'You yourself are the price to be paid for this sudden act of clemency from the Count. And you are prepared to pay this price.'

'No!' Doña Leonor cried. She attempted to raise herself, but sank once more to the ground. 'How can you believe', she struggled to speak, 'that I would... have betrayed... our love...'

Manrique, as the dreadful truth at last began to dawn on him, bent down to her and noticed creeping over her features the pallor of approaching death. He was struck with terror, and this terror, like a gust of wind, at once blew away all his feelings of hurt and jealousy.

'Leonor, what ails you?' he cried. 'Are you not well?'

From without they heard Azucena calling once more: 'What do you want with him? No, you must not take him! First let me speak to the Count!'

It was the sound of approaching footsteps that prompted her

to utter these words. The Count de Luna, followed by two men, had just entered the passage, intending, if need be, to have Manrique forcibly ejected from the gates of the palace. He had already reached the open door of the cell, but reeled back in consternation at the sight of Doña Leonor breathing her last.

Fortunately, she did not notice him. With an expression of total devotion she lay in Manrique's arms, and the loving, anxious look in his eyes as he gazed down at her filled her heart with peace and joy.

'It is the poison', she managed to speak with her last strength. 'There was so little time left... only a quarter of an hour... but now go... before the Count finds me like this... I would never... have... given myself... to another...'

Her head sank back, her voice failed. Manrique looked up at Don Nuño and the glances of the two rivals met in a look of mutual horror.

'The flask ...I suspected something', stammered the Count.

In desperation Manrique seized Doña Leonor by the shoulders and shook her. 'You must not do this!' he shouted. 'You cannot go like this! Not after I spoke such harsh words to you – not after I doubted your faithfulness!'

But the only answer Doña Leonor was able to give him was a smile of the most tender love – a smile which still remained on her face, as it became forever still.

Manrique lifted her up and laid her gently on his pallet. Then he fell down on his knees before her and buried his face in her shoulder.

For several moments no one was capable of speech. All that could be heard was the voice of Azucena calling from the passage way: 'Don't you dare touch a hair of Manrique's head – your master himself would not wish you to, once he knows what I have to tell him!'

Don Nuño entered the cell and looked down at the dead girl with burning eyes. 'You deceived me!' he hissed at her. 'So that is how you kept your word!' He stared around him, as if searching for someone to blame, and as his glance fell upon Manrique, he realized that he had found him. 'You!' he cried. 'You brought her to this! She wanted to gain your freedom? By God, you shall have it – in the same way as she has!'

At that instant he had made his decision and had also found the means of carrying it out. His raging pain drove all other considerations from his mind. He knew well that Manrique was a prisoner of the King, and should not be executed without royal consent, or a legal sentence. But now all of this meant nothing to Don Nuño. Even were he to tear asunder the world itself, he had to assuage his desire for revenge!

He turned swiftly to his men, and with the cool decisiveness for which he was known, issued them with instructions. The prisoner was to be executed immediately, by beheading, because shooting was impossible at such a late hour. In the adjacent courtyard, he told them, where numerous executions had already been carried out, there was a kind of scaffold and also they should be able to locate an axe somewhere. When everything was prepared, the entire escort was to assemble in the courtyard to witness the execution. They could draw lots to decide who was to carry it out.

The astonished soldiers, who had been ordered hither with entirely different instructions, hastened away to tell their comrades of the Count's will, and to arrange all that was necessary in order to fulfil it. They found the courtyard where the scaffold was, and after some searching they also found an axe that would be suitable for the dreadful purpose for which it was to serve. Then, while the rest of the men trotted sleepily to the place of execution, they once more climbed up the tower to fetch the prisoner – to deliver him, this time not to the freedom of life, but to that of death.

In the passage way a surprise was awaiting them: they heard the sound of singing, a man's voice singing. Manrique was singing a song to his dead bride. It was the song he had sung to her on that far off festival day, when they had first set eyes upon each other, and which had become from that moment on the song of their love: 'Time and space were lost to me, I saw you in eternity...'

The melody, carried by his deep feeling, filled the passage with its sweet sound; it resounded around the walls and moved the hearts of all who heard it. Azucena, although still standing at the bars of her cell, was silent, as if she had forgotten everything, her fear, her fever and her important message to the Count. The soldier who has holding aloft the torch, a simple, conscientious man, listened spellbound, with half open mouth. Even Don Nuño, to his own amazement, was deeply moved. It seemed as if his rival's voice was awakening some memory, an emotion which lay beyond all tangible understanding...

But the approaching footsteps of the soldiers, whom he had ordered to be the executioners of this singer, brought him back to reality. He saw Doña Leonor in the rigidity of death and forever removed from his possession lying on the other man's straw pallet. He saw the white gown, the ceremonial garment of death, which she had worn for the other man. He saw her pale lips smiling, as if she were even now enjoying the other man's singing; and this sight threw Don Nuño back again into that state of uncontrollable rage, that desire for revenge which excluded all rational thought. In a firm voice he ordered the soldiers to take the criminal to the scaffold and execute him at once.

Abruptly, the melody of the beautiful song broke off. Manrique looked up at the soldiers and smiled at them, as if they had come to fulfil his dearest wish.

'Soon nothing more can separate us', he addressed his dead bride tenderly, pressing her cooling hand once more. Then he fearlessly gave himself up into the hands of his executioners.

When the two soldiers led him past Azucena's cell, she realized that the fateful hour had come.

'Manrique!' she shrieked. 'What are they doing to you?'

'Farewell, mother!' cried Manrique. 'We will be reunited in a better world!'

'No!' Azucena screamed. 'Wait!'

But Manrique was already being led down the stairs by his guards. Azucena rattled the bars of her cell like someone demented and in rising terror she kept demanding to see the Count de Luna; she called out that she must speak to him, that she had something to tell him that would save Manrique!

The Count, who had stayed behind to gaze for the last time at Doña Leonor lying in Manrique's cell, decided to hear her, in the name of God. He tore the torch from the soldier's grasp and strode to her cell. 'What do you want, old woman?' he addressed her contemptuously. 'You cannot save your accursed son.'

Azucena was silent and stared at him, wide-eyed, through the bars of the door to her cell. 'The Count de Luna!' she cried. 'Heaven be praised, it is not yet too late!'

'For your son it is all too late', answered the Count grimly.

'No – listen!' Azucena called to him in haste. 'I wanted to wait until the trial before I spoke out, but now... Manrique is not my son. He is...' A shudder almost prevented her from speaking, but she overcame it and spoke quietly on: 'He is your own brother, Garcia.'

Don Nuño laughed out loud. He had expected anything, but not that. 'You are demented', he replied, in a tone that seemed a little unsure. 'It is the fever speaking, you crazy woman.'

'I know what I'm saying', Azucena insisted, 'and I can prove it. Look at me! Yes, I did have a fever, but now my mind is completely clear.'

The Count raised the torch to see her face more clearly and the laughter died in his throat. Certainly her face was marked by illness, and time and again as she spoke she began to lose the thread; yet in her terror-struck knowledge of what was at risk here, she summoned up all the strength of her mind, with an almost superhuman effort, thus endowing her words with an urgency that carried the ring of truth.

'He is your brother', she repeated. 'When, on that terrible day, when the fire... that fire... Yes, I wanted to kill him, but things turned out differently... What happened was that... my own child was burned, my own child...And so I took your brother in place of my son and brought him up – that is God's truth!'

Don Nuño stood, as if struck by thunder. He recalled his father's presentiments – recollected the remarkable similarity, which had even confused Doña Leonor, between himself and Manrique – thought of how, only a moment earlier, he had heard something in his brother's singing that triggered the voice of memory... Damn it! If this woman was telling the truth! Don Nuño rushed away headlong, and flew down the stairs, his heart pounding. He found the first courtyard deserted and hastened on, took a wrong turning, and raced back. At last he reached the courtyard which he had chosen to be Manrique's place of execution. Ghostly, in the flickering light of the torches he saw the hideous scaffold, saw his men standing to attention. Manrique, held by two soldiers, had already laid his head on the block. A third soldier held the axe high above his head and just at the moment when the Count yelled 'Stop!', it came whistling down onto Manrique's neck, abruptly severing his head from his body.

IX

Azucena survived her adopted son by only a few days. When she was brought the news of his death she lapsed into the harsh laughter of madness. 'Do you hear that, mother?' she rejoiced. 'Now you are avenged after all!'

She suffered a renewed attack of the fever, which brought on total insanity, and before the arm of earthly justice could reach her, she was already facing a higher judge.

The Count d'Urgell was forced to relinquish any claim to the throne of Aragon and sentenced to lifelong imprisonment by his victorious opponent. He lived in these unworthy conditions for more than twenty years, faithfully cared for by his wife, until at last death restored his freedom.

Don Guillén, the sole survivor of the de Sesé family, resigned his commission following the violent death of his mother, of which he could not feel himself to be totally innocent, and returned to his family estate to do quiet penance. His earlier ambition to win greatness and fame for the family he now saw to have been the source of its misfortune and he renounced it for ever. The rest of his life he spent working diligently and quietly at managing his estate, and in the course of the years achieved modest prosperity. Later, when he was in his mature years he started a family of his own, and in his old age he found consolation in seeing the proud hopes of his youth rekindled in several fine children and grandchildren.

The Count de Luna had to answer for the execution of Manrique Corda and the suicide of Leonor de Sesé, which soon led to investigations into his conduct during the storming of Castellar. The King was enraged when he learned how ruthlessly Don Nuño had abused his authority in order to follow his own personal vendetta and how unscrupulously he had set himself above the orders and existing rules of conduct. However, when in the course of the investigation, the details of the two deaths came to light, in particular the true identity of Manrique Corda, the King decided not to press formal charges against the Count de Luna; he clearly felt that this man, in view of these events, had suffered punishment enough. But from then on the royal favour was withdrawn from Don Nuño. He was obliged to leave the army ignominiously and was no longer received at court.

Upon his return to the Castillo at A. he once more led the life of a highborn gentleman, filled with hunting, parties and travel; but for the rest of his life he remained a man broken in spirit and was never able to get over the tragedy which deprived him of his brother and the woman he loved. Many times he thought back to the old gypsy woman's fateful words: You were born with many gifts yet you will have no joy of them. You will be rich, but you will never possess that which you most desire. You will live to be old but you will envy those who die young... How perfectly this prophecy had been fulfilled! How deeply he envied the dead the peace which eluded him! He travelled over the entire Continent, yet nowhere could he find anything that would give any meaning to his ruined life. He made the acquaintance of many beautiful women, yet none of them could bear comparison in his eyes with Doña Leonor.

Later in life he began to drink and to visit dens of vice. His fortune dwindled, his estate deteriorated. He spent his final years in poverty and total isolation at the Castillo in A., which had gradually become as dilapidated as he himself and which was regarded in the entire district as an accursed place, so that he was unable to turn it into money. As a result of his depravity he suffered from various different diseases, yet, as the old woman had foretold, he lived to a very, very great age.

At long last, when he was an embittered, decrepit old man of ninety-one years, death at last liberated him from his wretched existence. But even after that no one could be found who wished to live in his Castillo at A. Over the following decades, and then centuries, it crumbled away until it became at last the weathered and craggy ruin that greets the visitor today. Where once magnificent balls were held, wild grass grows through the cracks in the walls – where once you could hear shouts and the clattering of horses' hooves, now the only sound to be heard is the monotonous chirping of the cicadas. It is hard to believe that once upon a time this desolate place exercised a power that was felt in even the most remote villages of the area.

Content

Author and Project

Tanja Stern, born in 1952 in East Berlin, graduated in theatre studies, worked as an editor, bookseller, secretary etc. Her literary debut was in 1985 with The Trilogy of Losers. She lives in Berlin, writes novels, children's books, essays and film scripts. In her novel trilogy, Opera Murder she recounts the absurd plots of three well-known Verdi operas (The Troubadour, A Masked Ball, and Rigoletto) in the exalted language of the 18th century.

The Troubadour is part one of the novel trilogy. The other parts, A Masked Ball and Rigoletto, will soon be available in English.

A Masked Ball

Stockholm 1792. At a masked ball in the Opera house anti-royalist conspirators plan to assassinate the Swedish King Gustaf III. But at this ball, disguised in a mask and costume, Gustaf hopes to meet his secret love, Amelia, who is the wife of his most loyal friend. For this meeting the king throws all caution to the wind...

Rigoletto

Hide away what you love, otherwise it will be taken from you – this is a lesson that Rigoletto, the Duke of Mantua's crippled court jester, has long ago taken to heart. Full of suspicion, he keeps his daughter Gilda away from the dissolute court, without considering that by doing so he is attracting the Duke's curiosity about her...